Torgny Lindgren was born in No
the prize-winning author of novels, poems and short stories.
His works so far published in English include his novels
Bathsheba, *The Way of a Serpent* and *Light*, and a collection of
short stories, *Merab's Beauty*. His work is now translated into
25 languages.

Tom Geddes has regularly been Torgny Lindgren's English
translator. His translation of *The Way of a Serpent* was awarded the Bernard Shaw Prize.

Torgny Lindgren

IN PRAISE OF TRUTH

The personal account of
Theodore Marklund, picture-framer

*Translated from the Swedish
by Tom Geddes*

HARVILL
An Imprint of HarperCollinsPublishers

First published in Sweden in 1991
under the title *Till Sanningens Lov*
by Norstedts Förlag, Stockholm

First published in Great Britain in 1994
by Harvill
an imprint of HarperCollinsPublishers,
77/85 Fulham Palace Road,
Hammersmith, London W6 8JB

9 8 7 6 5 4 3 2 1

The author asserts the moral right to be
identified as the author of this work.

A CIP catalogue record for this book
is available from the British Library.

The Publishers gratefully acknowledge the
financial support of the Swedish Institute
towards the publication of this book in English.

ISBN 0 00 271255 5 (hardback)
0 00 271381 0 (paperback)

Photoset in Ehrhardt by Servis Filmsetting Ltd, Manchester

Printed and bound in Great Britain by
Redwood Books, Trowbridge, Wiltshire

N'importe où!
Pourvu que ce soit hors de ce monde!

BAUDELAIRE

I SAW HER AS soon as I came into the auction room in Ryda. She was hanging on the wall at the far end with a dozen pastels and landscapes in oil and aerial photographs of country mansions.

Now, long afterwards, I can almost imagine that she was calling to me over the heads of all the people in there.

I can't remember how I forced my way through to her: I must have pushed and shoved and kicked people on the shins as if my life depended on it. That's exactly the way you shouldn't behave when you're looking at items in an auction. But nobody took any notice of me. And nobody else seemed to have discovered her.

The Madonna with the Dagger. Though she wasn't called that then, of course; she didn't have a name. It was the journalists who eventually called her that.

She was dressed in a ruby-red gown, her golden hair was plaited in a circle over her forehead like a halo, her lips were slightly parted as if she was trying to say something but couldn't. She was a creature of beauty whose face expressed perfect purity. And she was holding the dagger in her right hand, the dagger that some art historians call a phallic symbol.

Of course I can't claim that I recognised her. Yet that is exactly what I have to say: I recognised her.

I know now that the dagger is fifteenth-century Moresque, made of silver and copper and in the Bishop's Palace in Senlis.

And I couldn't understand how a painting like that could have ended up here, in an auction room in a little village in our flat little corner of central Sweden.

The oil paint had that indescribable lustre and clarity that only one Swedish painter has ever achieved; it was like enamel.

7

She was standing before a city that seemed to consist almost entirely of churches, like a forest of towers and spires. On one of the church-towers the cross had been replaced by a serpent wearing a crown on its head. I could see it clearly when I took out my magnifying-glass.

It was an idiotic thing to do, using a magnifying-glass. You should simply appear indifferent at a pre-auction viewing. There are always people on the watch for others who might have made a find.

And at that very instant a bald-headed little man came and stood beside me.

"Lovely little thing," he said.

I said nothing. But I had a look at him. His face was exceptionally red and fleshy, with an expression of rather barbaric dignity. He looked like Gulliver in that watercolour that Dardel did for the Oslo exhibition.

"Bloody hell, she's lovely," he said.

And I remember him going on to say:

"It's strange, that, how looking at a painting can almost give you palpitations or make your pulses race."

He was saying it to her, not to me but to the Madonna, and it sounded as if he was accusing her.

Of course it's almost ludicrously difficult to talk about art. And about beauty. Beauty is a perversion – how can you retain your self-respect when you talk about it?

"Well, she's not really all that remarkable," I said, and stuffed the magnifying-glass back in my coat pocket.

"Have you found the signature?" he asked.

"It's unsigned," I replied. "It's probably a student work. From an art school in Gothenburg."

"I'm a widower," he said. It sounded as if he was introducing himself to the painting.

Then he asked whether I was an art-dealer.

"What would an art-dealer be doing out here in Ryda?" I responded. "There's only junk at auctions like these."

8

"But you're looking at the junk with a magnifying-glass," he pointed out.

"It wasn't intentional," I replied. "It's just a habit of mine. In fact you see things less well with a magnifying-glass."

"You're a collector," he said. "You collect art."

"I shouldn't think anyone collects art nowadays," I said. "Art has lost its value."

"Like hell it has," said Gulliver. "That's a bluff that the sharks in the art market have dreamed up. Those sods are trying to fool us."

"I'm a frame-maker," I said. "Stopped in the village on the way through. And I sometimes sell a picture or two."

I was thinking of my genuine oil paintings. I usually bought them ten at a time from a travelling salesman from Malmö. If customers wished, I could put lighting fixtures on them too.

"Actually, it was the frame I was looking at," I said. "It should be possible to mount something else in it."

It really was a remarkable frame. Hand-carved and gilded and two inches thick. Probably German, from the turn of the century.

"I'm absolutely certain I've seen her before somewhere," said Gulliver. "I'm not usually mistaken in such cases."

"There are always likenesses," I said. "There's nothing that doesn't resemble something else. All paintings are reminiscent of one another."

"I deal in just about anything," he went on. "Mostly cars. And old furniture."

"The furniture is over there," I said, and pointed towards the other end wall and the doors by the weighbridge.

"But I'm going to give up all this," he said. "I'm getting too old. You shouldn't try to handle big bulky objects when you're in your sixties. The only thing that matters is money."

We weren't looking at one another and we ignored the people jostling around us – our eyes were only on the Madonna.

"I've never even thought about money," I said. "When all's said and done, I don't know if there's anything that truly matters."

"When you get old," said Gulliver, "you realise that the only

9

thing that has any meaning in life is money. Money, that's the essence of existence."

I giggled, as I often do. It made me laugh to hear him use those words: 'essence of existence'.

"Money encapsulates everything," he added.

I don't know how long we stood there talking in front of the Madonna; neither of us wanted to leave the other alone with her. I can't give a verbatim account of all that we said because I'm having to write with my left hand now, and it's laborious, so I can only recount the most important parts. I'll explain later on how it came about that I can't hold a pen in my right hand.

That's one point I've forgotten to mention: there was something strange about the Madonna's left hand. It wasn't visible, it was outside the picture; it looked as if she was supporting herself against the frame or as if she was hiding something from us, some kind of secret that it hadn't been possible to paint.

I've occasionally thought since that I ought to have been honest with Gulliver. If I'd said that she was a masterpiece, that she was the first masterpiece in my life, then perhaps he wouldn't have been so suspicious, he would probably have realised that she wasn't for him.

Eventually he brought out a big square pocket torch that he'd had hidden in his clothes somewhere and switched it on and pointed the beam straight at her face.

It wasn't necessary. It wasn't at all dark in there. And her face glowed bright enough as it was.

So I grabbed his wrist with both my hands and twisted it till he dropped the torch and it fell to the floor and went out. "Don't bloody do that!" I yelled at him. "There are limits to what she ought to have to put up with."

And then I stamped on the torch a few times and walked away, ignoring him shouting at me to come back and the fact that all the people in the auction rooms had gone quiet and were staring at me.

Now I knew that I had only twenty-four hours to get some money together, as much money as possible, as much money as I could raise. The auction was to start at eleven on Saturday. Cash on the nail. That's a rule that can never be broken.

So now I must explain how I set about things when for the first time in my life I had to get some real money together. At the risk of confusing the reader, I have to preface this little account with a few words about my great-grandfather.

HIS NAME WAS Johan Andersson and he owned a place called Hill Farm at Raggsjö in the county of Västerbotten in northern Sweden.

In the spring of 1901 a missionary came to Raggsjö. Well, he wasn't exactly a missionary then, but he was going to be one. The only thing he needed was money. If he only had the money he would go to Africa.

He held four meetings and preached and collected two hundred crowns.

When he preached he wore a tail coat and high collar, everyone remembered that.

He left an address in Stockholm to which money could be sent in the future.

That was how the people of Raggsjö came to start the mission auctions. One in March and one in November.

On 18th November 1903 Johan Andersson purchased a black chest at the mission auction in Raggsjö. It wasn't particularly well made, the sides had mortice rather than dovetail joints, the hinges were crooked and it wasn't decorated or embellished in any way. My great-grandfather Johan Andersson was a good carpenter and would have been able to make a beautiful, perfect chest himself. But he wanted to show that he could excuse mistakes and bad workmanship, and that he even valued substandard efforts. He bought the chest as a token of his love of people and the world.

My grandfather was an only child, and so inherited the chest.

That was the only thing he inherited.

Great-grandfather Johan Andersson had given everything to the mission. At the end he owed seven years' taxes, and the state took the farm. He was sixty-three years old and a widower, and he moved into one of the outbuildings at Finberg's farm in Norsjö. He and that black chest.

On the underside of the chest, in the unpainted wood, he had carved these words: "Bought at the mission auction in Raggsjö 18th November 1903 by Johan Andersson. PRAISED BE THE LORD!" They are the finest-drawn and most beautiful letters I have ever seen.

But now I must tell the truth: he hadn't given quite everything to the mission.

Every now and then he'd put a coin or note in the chest. As if he'd thought: Perhaps there's a purpose that's even higher than the mission, perhaps even higher than God. You have to be prepared for everything.

He never touched that money, not even when the Crown took the farm. But if he happened to have some money in his hand at any time, a few coppers that he didn't need for the moment, he would put them in the chest.

And he taught my grandfather that that was how things should be, that when one day the chest was his, he in his turn should continue in the same way, never taking but only giving. All he was allowed to do was to change the coins for notes or the small notes for bigger ones so that there would be room in the chest for an unreckonable, even infinite, amount.

But what was the money for, Grandfather asked.

My great-grandfather said that that was something you could never know. It would become apparent when the time was ripe. A family could go on for generations, and then some day an absolute necessity would manifest itself, one fine day a descendant and heir would know that the moment had come and he would count the money and use it.

When my great-grandfather had only a few months more to live, the news came from Stockholm that the missionary was dead and so it wasn't worth sending more money. He'd never got to Africa: he'd died of drink in a restaurant called Dambergs.

Grandfather asked whether perhaps money would be needed for the funeral.

And then he said: "Everything that surrounds us is false, but we ourselves are genuine." That is the only utterance of my great-grandfather that has been preserved so that I can reproduce it word for word.

My grandfather moved south. If anyone asked where he lived, he just said: "In southern Sweden". He built a joinery workshop in an abandoned field full of thistles and mayweed – he got the money by marrying a farmer's daughter whom nobody else wanted. She was to be my grandmother.

He intended to make pianos.

His pianos were made of wood throughout. The strings were metal of course, but everything else, all the stops and mouldings and braces, was of wood. The frame was wood, and even the black keys.

He himself could only play one tune, and that was "Firmly I believe and truly, God is Three and God is One." But he didn't actually believe in anything. Except for this piano that he'd invented.

I was named after one of the sons of the piano-maker Heinrich Steinway: Theodore.

No finer instruments than Grandfather's have ever been made in Sweden. They looked like an eighteenth-century writing desk. There is one in the County Museum back home, with a portrait of Oscar II hanging above it. It's a very tasteful arrangement.

But the mechanics were somewhat unreliable and capricious. There was no obvious connection between the keys and the notes; if you hit a C, the piano was just as likely to respond with an F sharp. And it was impossible to tune Grandfather's piano. As soon as the piano-tuner finished and stood up you could play half a nursery rhyme and it would immediately be so discordant that the tune would break up and completely vanish. It was as if Grandfather had wanted to incorporate the totality of all the world's falsehood in one instrument.

The bankruptcy came as a liberation. The public prosecutor

withdrew the three charges for fraud and deception that Grandfather had brought upon himself. And the liquidator let him keep the mitre-box and moulding planes and a couple of saws and the set-square and mitre-plane and a carpenter's bench. That was how we came to be picture-framers.

But Grandfather never took a penny out of the black chest. And even though he'd lost everything, he would quite often find a little spare money to put in it.

My grandmother received an inheritance from America once. That ended up in the chest too.

Grandfather's pianos gave off an aroma. When you tried to play them and all the little parts were set in motion and rubbed against each other, a beautiful smell of pear tree and cherry tree wafted out. It was a fragrance that would bear comparison with almost any piano music imaginable.

But Grandfather was convinced that there must be someone somewhere who really could play his pianos. "You just need anticipation and guile to forestall all the tricks the piano thinks of," he would say.

He moved to our little village on the agricultural plain, and he and my grandmother rented the small green wooden house on the main road where the picture-framing business has been ever since. That was in 1929. They managed to buy the house a few years later. We've always been able to see Harmony Music Shop on the other side of the street through our two shop windows, and we've never been able to understand how that business was able to survive, with just accordions and guitars and recorders and sheet music, and the most unmusical area for customers in Sweden.

But people can't do without picture-frames. If there's anything they want to elevate or revere, then it has to be framed. A farmer in Fridhem had donated a hundred crowns to the politician Joseph Goebbels in Berlin, and my grandfather framed the letter of thanks. And reproductions and genuine paintings and mirrors and diplomas from the Agricultural Society and the Milk Marketing Board. We managed all right.

My father was born in 1936, an only child. We've always been only children. And widows and widowers and single people. As I write this I realise that different kinds of loneliness have always been quite usual in our family.

My grandfather was tall and slim and had sparse pale-blond hair. He looked like me. He read books by one author only: Arthur Schopenhauer. I've inherited his book collection: six volumes in worn, half-leather bindings.

My grandmother died in August 1938. She was taking a heavy gold-framed mirror to the vicarage in a wheelbarrow and she had a heart attack. She had a life assurance that paid out a thousand crowns, and my grandfather immediately put the money in the chest.

My father was only two years old. My grandfather looked after him, brought him up and made sure he got through school. And in the evenings and at nights he would sit in the framing workshop and make drawings and specifications for new pianos, uprights and grands, and even organs and strange musical machines which he invented and that others had probably already invented centuries before.

In the end I inherited all those drawings. I haven't thought about them for several years. I hereby donate them to the Science Museum in Stockholm. Or the Academy of Music. The last time I saw them they were in a box behind the rack of frame mouldings. The box had ELLOS LTD, Borås, on it.

When my father left school he started work in the picture-framing workshop. He was never a very good frame-maker. He applied the glue carelessly and often hammered the nails in askew so that the moulding split. All the time I was still in the framing business customers were constantly bringing back work that he had done long before and I had to do the whole thing again.

My mother came to the music shop as an assistant; that was how he met her. When the music shop changed ownership, in 1961, my mother was no longer needed and my father looked after her. Although really it was he who needed looking after. His health was

16

delicate and he was miserable and afflicted by painful twitches of the face – he often had to leave customers alone in the shop and go out to the back room to cope with the spasms on his own. He once won five thousand crowns on a penny lottery ticket that my mother bought him. But he had no dreams or expectations: all he had was a sense of duty. So he stuffed the money in the black chest and immediately forgot about it.

The inner room, the one behind the workshop, was where my grandfather lived. He'd moved there when my parents married. As he got old he began to shake his head, perhaps as a kind of counterpart to my father's wild grimaces, or perhaps because of some insight that had finally struck him. No one ever dared or even wanted to enquire.

It was Grandfather who was the major figure in our family's history. He formed the pinnacle: his pianos will endure. There is a person like that in every family, and all the rest of us are just padding.

I was born in 1964. But that didn't bring any great changes for us. Prints, particularly lithographs, had begun to be fashionable and in demand; we took in a lot of them for framing and my grandfather and Mother occasionally bought a few dozen themselves from the Art Promotion Society. It would have needed something much more dramatic than my birth to have made any significant alteration in our lives. Grandfather used to say that if anything changes, it's because something else has changed first. That was Schopenhauer, of course. And nothing else ever changed.

I was only three when Father died. It happened like this:

We had rats in the cellar. None of us ever went down there. When we – that is, Mother and Grandfather, not I, because I was hardly born then – when we opened the cellar door and listened at the head of the stairs, we could hear them, the rats, spitting and gurgling and snuffling, and we slammed the door shut again straight away. And there was a smell of ammonia and fermentation and decay. The only thing to do was to let the rats have the cellar in peace.

But it wasn't rats.

When Grandfather and Grandmother had moved into the house the cellar was full of glass demijohns. And they were allowed to stay there; they probably belonged to someone who might come and collect them. But as time went by my father secretly took them over and filled them with sugar and fruit juices and bits of potato and warm water and yeast: it was this brew that sputtered and murmured and stank so repulsively and ambiguously down there in the dark.

It's impossible to say when he started his brewing. He was probably already permanently inebriated when he met my mother. When the poison finally ended his life he was thirty-one years old. But Mother was never willing to recognise the truth. She always insisted most decisively that he died of those uncontrolled spasms and grimaces.

I've developed the habit of drinking aquavit myself occasionally. But only pure aquavit, unspiced, uncoloured and undiluted. Half a glass or so.

It was Grandfather who cleared up in the cellar. He piled the demijohns into the wheelbarrow and took them to the rubbish tip. I can remember nothing of all this, and I have no memories of my father. All my memories have come to me from my grandfather.

My mother never managed to recollect anything as it actually was, all her memories seemed to have a veneer of gold. When she left the music shop she was given a mandolin as a keepsake. She always said that it was an original. Grandfather had once swapped a bedroom mirror for a stained Wilton carpet, and that carpet was "a genuine Wilton". She used to say about my father: "He was such an upright and honest person." Every night as we were going to bed she would say: "I'm so pleased that you're having a really happy childhood." And just by her saying it, it almost became true. When she fell ill and Paula's mother told her that it might only be a cyst, Mother said – and it was just what I was afraid she would say – "No, it's an absolutely genuine tumour."

But she was a better frame-maker than my father. No one has ever complained about her work. It was actually she who taught me the profession. Grandfather used mostly to sit on a stool half asleep or talking to the customers or reading. He always had a pen and a ruler in his hand as he was reading, and the pages in the books I inherited are full of underlinings. I've never needed to read Schopenhauer from beginning to end, I've been able to restrict myself to the sentences and paragraphs that Grandfather had marked.

The black chest used to stand behind my mother's bed. It was usually called "the family fortune", sometimes "the inheritance". She had made a cover for it, of dark-blue velvet.

She died the summer I left school. My grandfather and I tried to sell the picture-framing business, but nobody wanted to buy it. We had decided that I was going to study in Gothenburg, and my mother had for several years called me her "little art historian", or sometimes even "curator".

Max Ernst died in the spring of the same year. *The Weekly News* printed his *Great Forest* on the centre pages. I sat for days just gazing at it. I didn't understand it, but it puzzled me in a pleasant way. Just as Mother had done.

I had no choice: I had to take care of my grandfather and the framing business. I did it for ten years.

Though I lost Grandfather after three.

I bought a car for the firm. An old Volvo Estate. And I also looked after the family chest. If it hadn't been for the art books, I would probably have been able to put aside more money than I did. Books on art are nearly as expensive as works of art. I eventually had two thousand volumes on painting and the graphic arts on my shelves.

And six volumes of Schopenhauer.

Many of the artists in nearby towns wanted me to help them sell their paintings. They wanted to hold exhibitions in the frame shop. But I refused, and kept to the genuine oil paintings that a travelling salesman from Malmö supplied me with. Really bad paintings are honest and genuine in a completely different way from mediocre serious art. I also got rid of the prints that Grandfather and Mother had bought from the Art Promotion Society.

It was really for art books that I'd gone to that viewing in the auction rooms in Ryda. They can turn up anywhere. I found Blunt's three volumes on Poussin at a sale of a schoolteacher's possessions in Brämhult.

W E'D GOT USED to the music shop across the road changing hands. A music business could get by for a few years, and then it was time to make way for someone else. We saw them come and go. Music was like that, it was fleeting and fickle, you could never rely on it. I was eleven when the Linnats took over the music shop. He was called Anders, but his real name was Andrzej; he had come to Sweden as a wartime refugee child. She was called Louise. She was expecting a baby.

He was well-built, red-haired and played the piano. It was summer when they moved in, and he often sat playing one of the two pianos that were in the shop. The door would be open and he would sing "*Aprite un po' quegli occhi*" and the Catalogue Aria in a voice that seemed to fill the whole district from the edge of the forest in the west to the motorway on the other side of the lake.

The baby was born in August. That was Paula. But her real name was Ingela; she didn't become Paula until twelve years later. And her surname of course was Linnat, even if it has never been spoken or written. No one has ever expected Paula to have a surname.

I'm going to call her Paula here. It's her real name now.

He gave piano lessons. The local newspaper did an interview with him. He had studied music in Copenhagen and Basle and Rome. He enjoyed teaching, although he wasn't a real teacher but rather a musician. In the newspaper photograph he was standing in front of the piano with his mouth wide open, obviously singing. He had a violin in one hand and a flute in the other. He'd done his best to bring with him into that one picture as much music as he possibly could.

Pupils came to him from the villages and industrial settlements throughout the area. It had to be completely silent in the house when he was giving his lessons. Paula's mother used to pick her up and come over to us. And the two of us, Paula and I, would crawl around on the floor, with me trying to teach her to walk and building strange little houses for her out of pieces of picture-frame moulding and cardboard boxes, and we would fill our mouths with wood-shavings and spit and blow at each other. We never thought about the fact that I was twelve and she just an infant – at least, I didn't – we were both equally energetic and lively and excited, and didn't think about anything in particular at all. Even then she had a distinctive, not to say peculiar, voice, as clear and strong as a flute, with an absolutely pure tone. She never shrieked like other little children, she just hummed and trilled and warbled as if she was practising scales.

I was so anxious to be near Paula that I got out my mother's mandolin and went over to the music shop to have lessons. Paula's father tore his frizzy red hair in a pretence of despair: he had never held anything as absurd and impossible as a mandolin in his hands before. But after that he really helped me; he showed me the right way to hold it and stuck a plectrum between my fingers and taught me how to produce a tremolo.

I can play "O Sole Mio" on the mandolin. And sometimes do so.

Of course I can't actually say that we grew up together, but I had a second childhood thanks to Paula, and it was more real and more genuine than my first. We had never truly existed before, together we formed something completely new: we were a clowning act or a secret society or quite simply brother and sister. I made puppets for us. We invented new plays for Harlequin and Colombine and Pantaloon and Pulcinella.

When did we start talking to each other? What was the first thing she said to me?

I don't know. In my memory we have always chattered and whispered and squabbled. The first words she learned she must have got from me and directed at me. It may have been "Till death us do part, Harlequin". I always made time to run across to Paula's for a while before I went to school in the mornings; and when I came home from school in the afternoons she would be standing waiting for me in front of our shop window with the genuine oil paintings in, or she might be sitting in the swing that I'd built for her in the pear tree in our garden.

Her father started teaching her as soon as she could hold a piccolo or sit still for any length of time at the piano. When she was three years old they played Schubert's A-minor sonata together, she at the piano and he with his cello gripped between his huge thighs. That was her first public performance. We were the audience, Mother and Grandfather and I and Paula's mother, and we had tea and cakes afterwards in their kitchen.

He would often come and fetch her just as we were building a snow castle or a hut made of branches or when I was in the middle of telling her a frightening fairy tale; music lessons were more important than anything else. Then I would sit on a piano-stool in a corner of the shop and listen to finger exercises and scales and all the études of Clementi and Cramer. He was impatient and bad-tempered and shouted, he seemed to be in an incredible hurry, driving and pushing her as if he only had a few months or at most a couple of years left in which to teach her everything a fully-fledged professional musician should know.

And that is in fact what happened. He disappeared when I was sixteen. Paula was five. It really did happen just like that: he disappeared. He took the bus into town one morning in April and was gone. He'd only intended to get his false teeth repaired. Paula's mother reported his disappearance, and for several days running we heard him being sought on the radio just before the evening news. He never arrived at the dentist's. Paula's mother said that he would have to reappear before long, because he couldn't go around for ever with that crack in his dentures.

I don't know whether Paula missed him. We never spoke about him. She continued to practise at the piano just as if he was still standing over her beating the time on her head. And I sat on my stool in the corner by the cupboard holding the music and the song-books.

23

Nor do I know whether Paula's mother missed him or yearned for him. She often spoke of the dreadful emptiness. And about how cruel it was to be rejected and deserted. And the fearful uncertainty. But you never knew what was genuine and what was false with her. She herself didn't know. She and my mother used to exchange magazines: *Swedish Women's Weekly* for *This Week*. I think she hoped she might find him again in a pictorial report of some big event, a concert or the opening of a golf course or a royal banquet. He would come back to her in a photograph in *This Week*. Because he was such a grandiose character with his passionate musicality and his enormous body and majestic red hair. And now on top of everything else that was unique or remarkable about him came his disappearance.

Fifteen years would pass before he showed himself again. And then only fleetingly.

Paula's mother continued to look after the music shop. As much as it needed looking after now. In a village of a couple of thousand inhabitants on a fertile plain there is no particularly great need for music. A social worker came twice a month with money for her. "Society has to support culture," Paula's mother said. "All of us involved in the arts are dependent on grants."

Then I began at grammar school and Paula started primary school. We read my homework together, history and German and social studies and history of literature, and she learned everything as easily and unconcernedly as I did. Her little body went to the primary school in the mornings, but her soul took the bus to the grammar school.

That autumn she sang in the church for the first time. You could see her red hair sticking up like the flames of a fire above the rail of the organ loft. Yes, Paula has red hair. Her hair is actually copper-coloured, even if no one would believe that nowadays. "Lead kindly light", she sang, "amid the encircling gloom, Lead Thou me on." None of us who heard her then can ever forget it.

It was about this time that we first saw Mr Crackshot; he was probably sitting in the church on that very occasion. He had been the district shooting champion in 1961, the three hundred metres

24

free rifle, and that was why he was called Crackshot. His actual name was Noldeby, everyone knew that. He was really born Andersson, but had taken the name of Noldeby. He'd once seen Emil Nolde's *Christ Receiving the World as a Gift*, and had been deeply moved; it was then he took the name Noldeby. He couldn't have known that that painting is probably a forgery. "There is no person and no act," says Schopenhauer, "that is without significance; the idea of humanity is manifest to greater or lesser degree in and through everything."

I didn't know who he was, but my mother had seen him before. He had been in *Swedish Women's Weekly* twice, once when a new restaurant was opened in Stockholm, and once when a pop-star had been buried. His name had been mentioned in the picture captions, but not his profession, presumably because he was so well-known that there was no need. We couldn't understand what Paula's mother had done to get a man like him to come. To her. To us.

But she told my mother about it. She had recognised him in *Swedish Women's Weekly*. They'd had a relationship when she was seventeen. That was her own word: a relationship. And now she'd found his address in the telephone book and written to him. About her life – no, not just her life: her pathetic fate. He came all the way from town in a taxi; we saw him get out of the car with a bouquet of flowers and a square package in his hands, walking with small, tripping, careful steps, since the first snow had just fallen. He was short and round and wore a large-checked overcoat; he looked like M. Delaporte in Toulouse-Lautrec's portrait. Paula's mother met him on the doorstep and embraced him and kissed him the way they do in women's magazines.

That evening we puzzled a lot about what might be happening in there. The lights were extinguished in the music shop, the curtains on the first floor were drawn. There must definitely have been wine in that package, Mother said. And caviar. And oysters. At ten o'clock the light in Paula's room went out, and an hour later all the windows were dark. The next morning a car came and fetched him. Paula stood on the steps waving as he drove away.

Paula and her mother were strangely secretive after that. Paula used to tell me everything. And my mother usually got to hear more than she really wanted from her mother. Paula had got a tape-recorder from him; that was what had been in the square package. She let me listen to a tape where she was singing "Ave Maria, maiden mild". Her mother had told her that Crackshot was Uncle Erland. And my mother was told that he was a director. Just director, nothing else. It had been wonderful to meet him again. Just think, after all those years. And it had felt as if all the time that had passed had been mere imagination and illusion, as if she'd been seventeen again, or eighteen at most. They'd drunk tea and eaten cheese biscuits and macaroons.

That was all.

"And," Paula's mother went on to say, "he knows absolutely everything about the world."

He came back, too. He kept on coming back, at intervals of a couple of months, always by taxi and with flowers and a package of some sort in his hands. He never showed himself outside the house except when he came and when he left. And we no longer asked about his business or what they really got up to behind the drawn curtains. He came to sleep with Paula's mother. That was it. They wanted to sleep together and she couldn't go to his place because she had her little girl. He had to come to her.

On two occasions he had an elderly woman with him. My mother said it must be serious now, she's got to meet his old mother.

But I asked Paula.

"It's a singing teacher," said Paula. "From Stockholm. She's teaching me to sing."

"You can sing already," I said. "No one has such a good voice as you."

"You have to practise all your life if you really want to learn to sing," Paula replied.

"But who's paying?" I asked. "A singing teacher from Stockholm."

26

"Uncle Erland," said Paula. "Whatever he feels like doing, he just does."

She was eight years old then.

It was that same spring that I took my school-leaving examinations. In June my mother died. Paula sang at the funeral. The cantor wanted to accompany her but she refused, her voice was enough on its own. "*Sie ist nur ausgegangen.*" I had tried to translate it; it was my translation she sang. I shouldn't mention such things. "She has but gone outside."

I transferred the subscription for *This Week* to Paula's mother. But she still kept bringing *Swedish Women's Weekly* when she'd read it. As if she didn't want to admit that Mother was dead.

I've realised subsequently that Paula was an unusual child. She went through her childhood impatiently and in a great hurry; she never gave herself time really to be a child. She would play with the dolls Uncle Erland brought for a few minutes, and then stow them away in a drawer in the loft the way parents finally do with toys that children have grown out of. And no little friends ever came to see her and run around giggling or playing with skipping ropes. She never read fairy stories. She played the piano. Or she would lock herself in her room with her songs and her breathing exercises. And we would sit together with our books, and often go to the village library together. We read at random and just for fun, novels and travel books and biographies and more or less anything we found. The important thing was not the books but the fact that we read them together.

When she was nine she was already getting little breasts that I didn't see; when she was eleven they were as big and as firm as they are now, but I still wasn't aware of them. Her whole body became that of an adult, but I didn't notice. She often helped me cut glass or picture mountings, and when we touched each other or bumped into each other I didn't feel how she'd grown rounder and softer, and I never realised that she no longer had the smell of a child.

The only thing about her that remained childlike was her face.

Everyone has seen it. Every single person in Sweden can call her face to mind at will. The maiden's pretty little face with the big eyes in Picasso's drawing of *The Minotaur and the Maiden*.

And I didn't understand what was happening to her voice. When we talked to each other I didn't hear that it had changed in some way. But she had begun to sing with an almost frightening boldness. I think I realised it during the early Christmas Day service the year she was ten. She was singing Beethoven's "Ode to Joy". Suddenly the hymn was about her personally, her voice itself was a message, a message that said: Nothing is impossible for me.

"*Froh, froh wie seine Sonnen fliegen, freudig wie ein Held zum Siegen, wie ein Held zum Siegen.*"

On 20th May of the following year Paula came over to me in the evening as I was standing holding a reproduction of Munch's *Scream* that I'd just finished framing, and said: "I'm going to move to Stockholm."

I said nothing; I couldn't understand what she meant.

"I can't stay here any longer," she said. "When you're as big as I am, you have to live in Stockholm."

That was actually what she said. She was no sacrificial lamb, not at that time.

"I'm going to live with Uncle Erland," she went on. "He's going to take care of everything. You don't need to worry. It's absolutely essential."

"Of course," I said. "It will turn out all right."

If I had understood what was about to happen, I would have opened the black chest that evening and counted out my family inheritance and taken it over to Paula's mother. I could at least have tried. Even if everything was already too late. But I understood nothing.

PAULA'S MOTHER had quite simply sold her to Uncle Erland. They had drawn up three different contracts – he, of course, had drawn them up; she had just signed them. In the first one she made over to him all her rights concerning Paula. In the second it was laid down how the revenues should be divided: seventy per cent to him, twenty per cent to Paula's mother, ten per cent to Paula. The ten per cent would be paid to Paula when she came of age. The third contract concerned the care of Paula: that was transferred entirely to him. He would be responsible for her board and lodging and schooling. Paula's mother received ten thousand crowns as a down-payment. And she said: "I mustn't think of myself and my own feelings, I must do my utmost for Paula and her future; I must make this sacrifice even if my mother's heart breaks."

I'll try to avoid writing about things that everyone already knows. Paula's mother cried with emotion all that night.

It was actually only then that Paula was first called Paula.

So he hadn't made his journeys in order to sleep with Paula's mother after all. Or perhaps he'd done that too, but only incidentally. It was because of Paula that he'd come, to keep his eye on her and watch over her so that no one else would snatch her away.

My mother had hoarded all those old magazines, they were in the loft. One evening after Paula had gone I sat up there and hunted out the issue that had Uncle Erland in it, burying a pop-star. There was also an interview with him, that Mother and I hadn't seen.

We had never understood how prominent and well-known he was, yet at the same time how shy and sensitive. He is known to everyone, it said, at least by name, even if it's not a proper name; he is the helper and fixer who is always in the background whenever

29

anything happens. He liked helping people, he said, it was in his nature. What he most frequently helped with was the sale and purchase of football players and pop-stars and ice-hockey players and artists, and even opera singers, writers and ventriloquists. There's nothing, he said, that compares with buying and selling talented people.

In her first letter to him Paula's mother had written: "I have a little daughter. I'm absolutely certain that she would be something for you. You ought to come here and have a look at her."

Paula and I found the letter much later. I have it now.

And he was always on the move, incessantly following up openings, opportunities, profitable possibilities. That was why he came.

I never got to know him. He will only be mentioned in this simple account when it is unavoidable.

I hardly need to describe what happened to Paula after that. No other child in Sweden has had such success. She was not even twelve years old when the whole thing began with that family show on TV one Saturday in November. When she later withdrew from her career, and thus also from her childhood, she was fifteen. They still play some of her records on the radio, and everyone who hears them stands up, goes quiet and says: "Listen! It's Paula!"

When a music critic compared her voice to a welding torch it was obviously not the hissing of the burning gas he was alluding to but the glow of the transparent jet of fire. Music represents pure will, according to Schopenhauer. I often think of that when I hear those recordings, whether country or rock versions of Schubert or Schumann or Mahler, or one of the songs that Uncle Erland got pop composers to write for her.

What did I do during all those years? What did I achieve while she broke one public record after another and won the Eurovision Song Contest and sold fifteen million discs?

I looked after the picture-framing business.

And I talked to her on the telephone; we spoke to one another every day. It was mostly she who rang, sometimes from the one-room flat that Uncle Erland had got for her in Stockholm, more often from Gothenburg or Malmö or Copenhagen or Hamburg or London or wherever she might be. We felt compelled to tell one another that we were happy and that everything that was befalling us was incomprehensible and grotesque and like a fairy tale, and that we missed each other and would soon meet again.

When I was twenty-three I lost my hair. I thought it was quite natural, and I never went to the doctor. It took three months. I kept a narrow circle of curly down at the back and above my ears. When I told Paula about it, she said it was because I read Schopenhauer. "But I read other things, too," I pointed out. Yet I had a feeling that in some way she was right.

I've always regarded myself as an intellectual. I've sometimes amused myself by thinking: "I'm the only intellectual picture-frame maker in the whole of Sweden."

We never met. Paula didn't have time, Uncle Erland wouldn't let her, I was too cowardly to go to her.

But her mother went to Stockholm a couple of times a year and hugged her and collected her money. And they were splendid times for her music shop; she sold the sheet music of Paula's songs and photographs of Paula when she was an even younger child than now – she signed them herself – and piano stools that she called Paula's piano stool and recorders and guitars and flutes, even ocarinas that had all been Paula's. Whenever you met her she would be constantly lamenting her inability to drive: she would so much have loved to buy a Mercedes or a Jaguar.

Grandfather used to complain about being so alone. My mother and father were gone and I wasn't concerned with anyone except my little friend, Paula. Now I understood what he'd meant. And the next year I tried for three months to experience what it was like not to be alone. This is how it came about:

I had to frame an illustration from *True Story*. Paula's mother wanted it done; she said she was going to give it to one of her sisters.

She had given me the whole magazine. It was a bathing beach, a man and a woman kissing against a background of rippling green water. When I'd cut out the picture and mounted it, I read the magazine. And I found this advertisement: "Are you waiting for something grand and stupendous in your life? Do you want something absolutely incredible to happen to you? Replies to Lena, 25."

I wrote an answer. Two weeks later she was with me. Her name wasn't Lena at all, it was Maria.

I told Paula about her, on the second evening of her stay with me, and Paula said: "That's exactly what you need."

Why she chose to come to me I don't know, I never asked. She had been living with a strawberry-grower in Fjugesta, and before that with a lorry-driver in Karlstad. She had also lived with a post-man, a baker and a dental technician. But she had never tried a picture-frame maker.

She was tall and slim and had sorrowful eyes. The eye shadow she used was mother-of-pearl. She had never trained for any job. But she was inquisitive and interested when I was at work. I had mentioned in my letter to her that I knew Paula: perhaps that was why she chose me. She carried on putting her advertisement in various magazines, always the same advertisement, and she would sit for days on end reading through the letters she received and answering them. "You should always be ready to start all over again," she would say. "It's dangerous to settle down. Life is stuffed full of discoveries and bargains and lucky gambles, it's just a matter of keeping an open mind and holding yourself in readiness."

A few weeks before Christmas she moved in with a funeral director in Västerås. "You never know," she said. "This could be something special." By then I had almost come to like her.

No one could understand why Paula stopped. She herself wanted to continue, the power of her singing was the same as ever, perhaps even stronger. And her public was certainly not deserting her.

For several weeks in January the newspapers were full of articles about her disappearance, as they called it. They wrote of the ever-mounting expectations of her audiences and about the probability of her advanced state of pregnancy. One magazine launched a competition: What would the name of Paula's baby be? But the journalists' stores of inventions and lies were soon exhausted, her name stopped appearing on the billboards, and it seemed as if they had simply come to an agreement to forget her for a while at least.

But Uncle Erland knew what he was doing, of course. He'd put her in quarantine. He'd realised that it was no longer possible to convince the public that she was still a child. In the long run no little-girl dresses or ribbons and bows or cherub's curls could hide the fact that she was a grown woman. He made her withdraw before anyone discovered that as a child she was a fake.

Paula rang me and told me that she wasn't going to be allowed to sing any more now; she was crying. For a short while I imagined that I might get her back again.

But things weren't that simple. As everyone knows by now.

She was to be kept out of sight of the world for three years. No public appearances, no interviews, no tours. He moved her to a little flat in another part of Stockholm; if she ever left it she had to wear an enormous blond wig and glasses. The restaurant next door, the Jester, used to deliver meals to her twice a day.

The idea was that when the three years had passed she would be resurrected. Or something like that. And then she would be completely transformed.

Everything Uncle Erland did was thoroughly thought out and minutely scrutinised from all angles. He really took care of her. He hated anything fortuitous or accidental. Paula's mother told me she thanked God every night for the fact that she'd been able to put Paula's life in such safe hands.

He arranged for another of his young singers to come one evening a week and play cards with her. I don't know her name; Paula called her the Watchful Eye. Probably nothing much ever came of her.

And he formed Paula Music Ltd, in which he himself owned all the shares. "Now no one will be able to cheat you," he said.

He bought a school-leaving certificate for her from some private school, God knows where.

Teachers came to her every day and gave her tuition. Dancing. Deportment. Singing. Perhaps karate, too. Or some other kind of self-defence, I can't remember.

And he employed her in Paula Music Ltd. She received a monthly salary and contracted herself to stay with the firm for ten years.

Everything was a preparation for her second career, the definitive and genuine career.

And on her eighteenth birthday she got her money, exactly as laid down in the agreement with her mother. She told me about it the same evening. He had arrived with red roses for her. "This is an extremely important moment," he had said. "Now you're your own mistress."

But then we went on to talk about something else: I'd sent her a biography of Picasso, which she'd read.

When I got home from the auction rooms at Ryda where I'd seen the Madonna, I took out the black chest, lifted off my mother's velvet cover, and opened it.

Then I counted out the money. I poured it out on the big table that I used for cutting the picture-mountings. It was really not just myself counting it but all of us – Great-Grandfather and Grandfather and Grandmother and Father and Mother. And me. We had never counted it before. It amounted to 93,451 crowns and 95 öre.

I slipped the five-öre coin under the cork mat, at a join. It brings luck.

It was a lot of money. It was far more than could be expected of a family that had constantly lost everything.

But it still might be too little.

The human world is a realm of chance and illusion, according to Schopenhauer. Chance rules us mercilessly.

That was why I rang Paula.

When I said that I needed money, Paula didn't ask why. We had never spoken about money before.

"I think I've got masses," she said.

"It's Friday today," I said. "The banks are closed."

"I've got it here," said Paula. "In a box with my glove-puppets."

When Uncle Erland had asked her how she wanted to have her money, she'd said: "I'll have it as it is." And he'd brought it in an envelope and she'd rolled it up and stuffed it under Columbine's skirt.

"But I've never counted it," she said.

When I told her about the Madonna I'd found, she said: "You don't need to explain anything."

So I waited while she took the box out of a wardrobe and counted the money. I could hear that she was playing Wagner – Uncle Erland had given her a stereo player – something from *The Valkyrie*.

It's the most fake music I know.

It came to 32,500 crowns.

I thought of the enormous sums of money that the newspapers had ascribed to Paula.

"If I take the last train of the evening," said Paula, "I should get there."

"Will he really let you do that?" I asked.

"No," she said. "But I can see that it's necessary. And I rehearse during the day."

I met her off the train at five in the morning. I hadn't seen her since the evening she sang on television for the last time: Schumann's "Silent Tears". She was accompanied by some backing vocalists and a synthesizer. I think my grandfather was still alive and he wept. Or it might have been me.

If she hadn't been wearing that big blond wig and the dark glasses

35

that she'd mentioned, I wouldn't have recognised her. She had the box of glove-puppets under her arm.

We drove home to my place. I'd made the raspberry fool that she always wanted when she was small. When she'd given me the money and I'd put it in the black chest, we tried playing with the glove-puppets. But it was no good. She could only stay for two hours before she had to catch the train back to Stockholm again. I wanted to give her a receipt for the money, but she refused to take it. She didn't touch the raspberry fool. She didn't feel up to driving out to see Grandfather's grave, she was pale and looked as if she was freezing cold.

We'd be able to speak to each other on the telephone again when she was back in Stockholm.

And we couldn't go over to the music shop and wake her mother. She didn't want to meet Paula during this period. She had said: "I want it to be a surprise for me. What sort of person you are and what you look like when you emerge from your chrysalis and are grown up. You mustn't begrudge your little mother that pleasure."

When I got back home after taking her to the train I transferred all the money to Grandfather's leather briefcase. 125,951 crowns 90 öre.

And as I've said, the auction was due to begin at eleven o'clock.

M ONEY IS the only true representation of all the good in the world, Schopenhauer says in *On Ethics*. I was thinking of that as I drove out to the auction rooms in Ryda.

Auctions like those always begin with the simplest items; they're knocked down quickly, almost carelessly – rag rugs and imperfect chairs and sewing boxes and ancient unusable tools. This warms up the bidders, they imagine that bargains are to be had. After a few minutes the auctioneer slows the pace – by that time he's up to the lamps and porcelain and glass – and he gets more serious and never lets the hammer fall until he is sure he has heard the last and highest bid.

They would probably get to the paintings after a couple of hours.

I arrived at a quarter past eleven. The car park was only half full. I was completely calm. But a little on the warm side, as if slightly feverish.

Gulliver was standing on the stairs, the man who dealt in anything and everything. He'd been waiting for me. We didn't exchange greetings, we pretended we hadn't even seen one another. I was carrying my briefcase with both hands, holding it pressed to my stomach. As I approached, he turned round slowly and opened the door and went into the auction hall, his right hand patting the wallet that was sticking up out of his back pocket.

It struck me that I actually knew nothing about money, and he probably knew everything.

Perhaps I would get her for five hundred.

It was the usual old auctioneer, a shrill, red-haired chap who had run the village shop in Ryda a long time ago. The audience was also the usual crowd, people who feel duty bound to go to every auction.

I recognised the backs of their heads and their quilted jackets and sheepskin coats as they stood facing the auctioneer. Seventy-five to eighty people, no more. And when they turned round every one of them knew me.

Gulliver went straight over to the Madonna. And there he stayed, probably wanting to show me that she was his and that I shouldn't make assumptions. I stood with the others. I inspected the faces one by one to see whether there were any strangers there, anybody who might be an antiques dealer or art dealer or even simply a Stockholmer. But I couldn't see anybody.

I didn't look across at the Madonna. I didn't begrudge Gulliver that pleasure. But I wondered what I would do if he took her from me.

I bent forward from time to time and let the briefcase rest against my thighs. It wasn't just notes, there was nearly two thousand crowns in one- and five-crown and fifty-öre coins.

Everything was going fairly cheaply. The dearest purchase was a grainy corner cupboard, at 3,200.

We got to the paintings at one o'clock. The landscape oil paintings went for seventy-five crowns each. I usually sold them for four hundred or six hundred in the picture-frame shop. Then the auctioneer said: "And here we have an oil painting by an unknown artist. What am I bid for the lady?"

It was the Madonna.

There was silence at first. Then someone said:

"Twenty-five crowns."

I was suddenly afflicted with a fit of shivering; a strange tremor went through my whole body so that I nearly dropped the briefcase. I gave a laugh that made everyone turn and look at me. I could hear myself how shrill and excited the laugh sounded. I had to say something.

"One thousand crowns," I bid.

Then there were just the two of us, Gulliver and I.

"One thousand five hundred," he said.

And I said: "Two thousand."

When we reached five thousand it was completely silent all around us; I didn't notice it then, but I remembered it afterwards. All eyes turned from him to me and back again as if our battle were a tennis match.

When he bid 30,500 I tried to shake him off me.

"50,000," I said.

"50,500," he bid.

Then I realised that he knew. He had recognised the colouring and the brushwork and the lines in her face and the sure, firm contours. He was going to snap up a bargain, it was the profit-motive driving him.

We went on to raise the bidding by five hundred or a thousand each time according to whim or the sound of the sum itself when we imagined ourselves saying it. 84,000 has a finer ring to it than 83,500. It was our way of testing one another; he was trying to work out how much I had in my briefcase, and I was estimating how much he might have in that thick wallet in his back pocket. I remember thinking that when he carried her out of there I would knock him down and tear her out of his hands and run off with her, anywhere.

And what if Paula had made her night-time journey and given me all her money in vain?

120,000. 120,500. 122,000.

Finally we reached 125,000. That was his bid. Now I've lost, I thought. I should have realised that I wouldn't be a match for this. He's going to drive straight down to Stockholm and sell her. But I said: "125,500."

Gulliver didn't say 126,000. The auctioneer repeated my bid and looked over to him and waited, but he was silent and stared down at the ground – I couldn't resist looking at him at last. The furrows on his brow and bags under his eyes were quivering. In the end he raised himself to his full height, stretched out his arm and pointed at me.

"Don't believe him!" he screamed. "He hasn't got the money! The bastard's trying to bluff us!"

So now we knew how much he had in his wallet. And the

39

auctioneer did his job and started the court: First time, second time, third time. Then he brought down the hammer on the block and the whole thing was over.

There was still complete silence in the hall as I went up to the auctioneer's assistant, the cashier who had an old bus conductor's money satchel hanging over his belly, an anxious and solemn silence. I opened the briefcase and took out 451 crowns 90 öre and put that in my pocket. Then I handed the briefcase to the cashier.

"That should be right," I said.

At first he seemed somewhat confused. I don't know what he'd expected, perhaps that I would bring out the money in neat bundles. But then he took the briefcase and went over to an old kitchen table which hadn't yet been sold, turned the briefcase upside-down and carefully shook out all the notes and coins.

At that the people in the auction hall started to cheer, they applauded and whistled and stamped their feet as if the cashier and I had performed some great magic trick, as if that heap of money was the most beautiful and most exciting thing they'd ever seen. It took a good while to count it and the applause went on the whole time. Finally the cashier straightened up and said:

"Yes. It's right."

I turned round and bowed. I don't know why I did it. I wanted to thank the audience for their ovation, on behalf of the money and my family and Paula.

Then I lifted the Madonna down from the wall.

"You can keep the briefcase," I said to the cashier.

I think Schopenhauer said: "Everything that is perfect is almost unbelievably light." But she was heavy, much heavier than I'd expected. And I'd dealt with paintings all my life. She has since been weighed, of course, and now I know: she weighed 16 kilos 83 grams.

I'll never forget how it felt to press her to my breast. My arms were shaking a little – I'd been carrying the briefcase for several hours, after all. I'd never expected anything overwhelming to happen to me. Paula was the only grand or exceptional or delirious event in my life. Now even as I'm telling the story I still feel somehow that from this point on I should write in a different way, in a more elevated and soulful style; mediocre, everyday language makes the account seem in some way false or mendacious.

When I came out to my car, Gulliver was standing waiting for me. He had slipped out of the hall without my seeing him, he hadn't stopped to applaud my money.

"I suppose I should congratulate you," he said. "Despite everything."

"Thank you," I replied.

"Who are you buying for?" he asked.

"Nobody," I said. But then I changed my mind and added: "For my family."

"Are you going to sit on her or cash in your profit right away?"

"She will never be sold."

I wrapped her in two blankets before I laid her in the car.

"I wonder who the painter was," he said.

"Don't you know?" I was so amazed that I looked him straight in the eyes. They were so screwed up and rheumy that they were hardly visible.

"How the hell should I know that?" said Gulliver. "I'm not an art-dealer. I'm not even a picture-framer."

"If you didn't know," I said, "how could you bid 125,000?"

"I saw the look on your face when you first caught sight of her," he said. "When you've been at it as long as I have, you can count the money in people's faces."

"How much did you see in mine?"

"Half a million," he said. "Roughly. But 125,000 was all I could scrape together over the weekend."

"It wasn't money you saw," I said. "It was something immensely greater and more lasting."

That was as far as I felt I could go. I didn't want to have recourse to any more pompous words than these.

"There is nothing greater or more lasting than money," said Gulliver.

Then I thought to myself: He might just as well know. I can allow him that much.

"It was Dardel who painted her," I said. "Nils Dardel. Nils von Dardel."

"Who the hell is he?" he asked.

I didn't really know what to say then. But I replied:

"He is the greatest artist Sweden has ever known."

"Well, well," said Gulliver. "Well, well."

The last thing he said before I got into the car and drove off was: "You must never imagine that I'll forget this. No, don't think that for a moment."

I drove slowly. I don't think I once dared to change up to top gear. And suddenly I heard myself sitting there singing. I almost never sing. An old hymn that my grandfather had taught me a long, long time ago:

> "The strife is o'er, the battle done;
> Now is the Victor's triumph won;
> O let the song of praise be sung.
> Alleluya!"

I PUT HER DOWN on the sofa beneath the window. I sat for a couple of hours just gazing at her.

Then I rang Paula. When she answered I found it almost impossible to say anything, my emotion had robbed me of my voice, and I just whispered my story to her. "We now own a real Dardel, unsigned, admittedly, but a fantastic painting; we're the joint owners of it, you and I."

"If you say it's a Dardel," said Paula, "then it must be. The way you describe it, it sounds as if it's an unusually small painting. As if it were cut down in some way."

"No," I whispered, "it isn't cut down, it's just so powerfully dense and compressed, it's like a diamond."

And we laughed together and blew down the telephone at one another.

Paula was tired, she'd been working in the studio the whole day, she and the new composer and the musicians and technicians, and Uncle Erland – they'd slaved and toiled every day, weekdays and weekends, over the previous month; she was to appear on the stage again a week later, it was time for her to crawl out of her chrysalis. There was going to be a live television broadcast of half the performance.

"I'm sorry," I said, "I'd almost forgotten about that."

"The whole thing feels like a miracle," said Paula.

"Yes," I said. "Who could have imagined all this? About you and me."

"Can't you come and stay with me?" Paula asked.

"I've got my business to look after," I said. "And why should I come and stay with you?"

*

When dusk fell I carried a daylight lamp and reflector over from one of the shop windows and fastened it on the arm of a chair so that the light shone on her from the right-hand side, slightly from above. The colour was even clearer, the sheen more lustrous.

I felt a childish and ridiculous urge to show her to someone, anyone at all. So I rang Paula's mother. She came at once.

"Oh, how charming and delightful," she said. "She looks like Paula."

"I can't see the likeness," I replied.

"But who can have painted it?"

"Dardel," I said.

"Oh, of course," said Paula's mother, "that was exactly what I thought."

"You can't mistake a Dardel," I said.

"No, definitely not," she agreed. "It's only Frenchmen who can paint like that."

It was a relief when she went and left me alone with the Madonna again. "I must hurry back home," she said, "Paula might ring at any time."

Paula never ever rang her, I knew that for a fact.

Someone once said that every need or lack or suffering gives rise to a desire, and that when such desire wanes or is satisfied countless others remain. And that desires persist indefinitely and are unmeasurable, whereas pleasure is brief and limited and only illusory. From satisfaction new desires grow.

I thought to myself: That's not true. I'm satisfied.

In that powerful oblique beam my eyes caught sight of a join or dark line on the outer edge of the frame. It was strange. It looked as if the frame consisted of two frames laid one on top of the other. That was done sometimes. To achieve depth or weight or rigidity. But the Madonna didn't actually require it.

Yes, I thought. Of course. That's it.

I took out the little chisel that I always keep in my pocket and started to test it carefully. It definitely was a line or a slit. In a couple of places the gold leaf covered the join, and it broke. I've never really

44

believed that one thing conceals another, nor did Paula and I play games like that, and I've never expected the unexpected. But I thought to myself: I must at least have a look to see how this frame has been made.

So I laid the Madonna on the coffee table and fetched a knife and a strong chisel.

The two halves were fixed together with pegs. It was well done. But none of it was glued, so it wasn't difficult to widen the gap millimetre by millimetre and finally lift the back frame off.

What I saw was incomprehensible. There were four panels. Three of them were fastened together with small brass hinges, and the hinge was raised on one side with a thin strip so that the three panels could be folded together over one another. The fourth panel was just a protection for the other three.

I thought I was working very fast. If anyone had asked how long it took me to prise up the frame and open out the entire painting and reveal it all, I'd have said about two or three minutes, no more. But when I finally sat down and looked at the complete Madonna and also quickly glanced at the clock, I discovered that it was already morning – it was five o'clock. I had worked so slowly and carefully with my hands, and also stood still for long periods with my arms just hanging at my sides, that it had taken me six hours to do.

Yet in fact the whole thing was in a way so simple, even obvious.

The Madonna was a triptych. It was painted on canvas and the canvases had been mounted on very thin panels of pear-tree wood. When the three parts were unfolded, when you opened out the whole picture, so to speak, the joins no longer showed. It was 80 by 150 centimetres.

Virtually everyone knows now what it looked like, of course.

The central piece, the Madonna herself, the part that had appeared to be the whole work, I have already described. The right-hand side piece was covered in its upper half by a cobalt-blue sky, and the sky was adorned with images and signs that can only be described as ornaments: doves and heavenly bodies and comets and flags, and on one of the flags I could read with a magnifying-glass the words BLOOD and FIRE In the Madonna's left hand that had been hidden under the frame there was a cross, and on the cross hung a Christ who was not the usual crucifixion figure but the little child to be seen in every other painting resting against his holy mother's breast. She was holding the cross in a preoccupied, rather absent-minded way, as if she didn't really know what she should do with it, and lower down the cross merged into an anchor. The left-hand side piece was overflowing with spectators, all with their eyes fixed on the Madonna. Many of them were easily recognisable, they were Dardel's fellow-artists – one of them was Jean Cocteau – and friends and relations and art dealers of whom he had painted portraits elsewhere. There was Gulliver too in the middle of the crowd, together with the Man from Uri. And there, on the left-hand side piece, was the signature: Nils de Dardel 1919.

I should have folded her up again and put her back in the frame and stuck the two halves of the frame together with glue. But it never occurred to me. The only thing I could think of doing was to sit absolutely still and just gaze at her. I forgot that the whole night had passed and that I really had a duty to myself to sleep; I didn't become either hungry or thirsty; I didn't feel that I had any needs at all.

Over the last few months I've read several books by André Gide; Paula gave them to me. I wish that I could write like him. Then I would have recounted the feelings that went through me, joy and amazement that were almost a kind of intoxication, and confusion and excitement that prevented me from getting up and doing anything other than sit staring like a madman. Now there's any number of newspaper articles and essays about the *Madonna with the Dagger*, about her origins and adventures and her unique place in Dardel's oeuvre, and of course about all the possible meanings contained or concealed in the three parts of the painting, and about the heart-rending or possibly jocular or even offensive message that she conveys. Everyone who sees her creates a personal interpretation, she can obviously mean anything at all. I know what Dardel wanted to express. I saw it at once, that was what I sat staring at on that first night. But I shall not say it.

Eventually I heard someone knocking on the shop door, power-ful blows with the palm of a hand. I came to myself again at last, and stood up and ran down to open it. It was twelve o'clock.

"It's Sunday," I said. "I'm closed today."

It was the farmer from the big yellow house by the river. I've never bothered to distinguish between open and closed, customers have been at liberty to come whenever they happened to have the time. And he knew that.

"I just wanted to bring in this matchstick picture," he said. "The matchsticks are beginning to come loose: I'd like to have glass put over it."

I took the picture and held it carefully the right way up. It was of a windmill on a hill by a lake. I've always felt an affection for matchstick pictures which is hard to explain. They are much more fragile than you'd think, they have to be handled very care-fully, and it's unusual to find works of art made with such love and care.

Then I worked all day on the new frame for the Madonna. I used the same French moulding that I'd had for the reredos in the church at Fridhem. That's the frame that has since been seen in all the newspaper photographs. I'm convinced that Dardel himself would have chosen exactly that shape and the matt gold colouring.

I phoned Paula and tried to tell her what had happened, what I had found inside the old frame. She just laughed at me, incessantly and almost angrily. She still does today when she reminds me of that conversation. Everything I said seemed totally incomprehensible to her. She thought the painting had torn and that I couldn't repair it and that I was sitting there with three separate pieces or fragments in my hands. She maintains that I just kept saying that what had happened was dreadful and inexplicable and an irreparable mistake. That can't be true. In fact the only thing she had in her head was her own rehearsals: she was anxious and tense and excited. I'm pretty certain that I even asked her what sort of music she was working on and that she said it was gospel, the earliest form of gospel music imaginable.

The newspapers had carried the first articles about her re-appearance a few weeks earlier. "She'll hit us like a megaton bomb," they said. "The most remarkable transformation in the history of the Swedish entertainment industry." But everything was very secretive, and no journalists had been allowed to meet her.

When the Madonna was framed I cleared out the right-hand shop window and put her there, supported by small trestles and with lamps shining on her so that the light was evenly distributed over the three parts. From outside on the street she really looked like an altar triptych. I brought down a mattress, a pillow and a blanket and made a bed for myself on the floor. Then I slept with her, behind her back, as it were.

I WANTED EVERYONE TO SEE her and yet I hoped that no one would notice her.

It was actually only my neighbours who had reason to pass by on the pavement outside. And I don't know whether they usually looked at my windows. They'd known for a long time what there was to see, they would know in advance what the new pictures would look like even before I put them in the window.

The first person to discover her was the local editor of the county newspaper. He'd done an interview with Paula's mother. He didn't even bother with a greeting when he came striding in. I was sitting at my bench glueing in matchsticks on that windmill picture.

"Fine painting you have in the window," he said.

"It's a Dardel," I replied. "A triptych."

"Who's Dardel?" he asked.

"The greatest Swedish artist of all time," I said. "Nils von Dardel."

"That's not what's on the painting," he responded. "It says Nils de Dardel."

"His family came from Switzerland," I said. "French-speaking Switzerland."

"It's a reproduction," he said.

"She's genuine," I replied. "She's as genuine as any art can be."

He was silent for a moment. He went over to the window and leaned over and looked at her from above.

"Then it's probably worth a hell of a lot of money," he said.

I can't understand it now, afterwards, but I hadn't once thought about what she might be worth. For me the Madonna had nothing to do with money, not even with the family inheritance from the black chest.

49

"That's irrelevant," I said. "I won't ever be selling her."

"Art," he said, "that's the best security there is. I know a photographer in Örebro who's got a painting that's supposed to be worth fifty thousand crowns."

I said nothing. He wouldn't understand me, no matter what I said.

"Holds its value," he said. "Like land and forests. Appreciation. Bricks and mortar. But not prints and drawings. And not matchstick pictures, either."

He went on in this way for some time. I didn't listen. In the end I said:

"Many years ago a Dardel was sold at auction in Stockholm. *The Dying Dandy*. That's also a masterpiece."

"The dying what?"

"Dandy."

"And what did it go for?"

"I can't remember," I said. "I've never thought about it since. Several million."

He was quiet for a while. Then he said: "You're pulling my leg."

"I don't know how to go about pulling someone's leg," I said. "I've never done it in my life. No one taught me how to do it. I've often wished I could."

This was quite true.

"Several million," he said.

"Yes," I said. "Several million."

"And what's it called, this painting?"

"I don't know," I answered. "It doesn't really need a name. It's meaningful enough in itself."

"I don't think I understand that," he said.

"Perhaps I misunderstood your question."

"Is this one as good as that other one?"

"It's better," I said. "It's the most remarkable Swedish work of art of our times."

"You're sure of that?" he asked.

"Yes, I am."

50

He was forced to think for a moment.

"But there's one thing I don't understand: how the devil did you come by it?"

"I bought it," I replied. "With my own money. Cash."

I wasn't going to mention Paula.

"I'd better look him up," he said. "In the library. Dardel."

Then he wanted to take a photograph of me and the Madonna. To be on the safe side, he said. In case there might really be something in this story. So I turned her round and climbed up into the shop window and stood behind her, and he photographed us.

As I stood there holding the top of the frame I said something rather strange; I don't know why I said it, but it went so uncomfortably quiet while he was getting the camera ready and I probably thought I ought to look as if I was speaking on the photograph: "It's this painting that's the meaning of my life."

I didn't think he would put that in the newspaper. But he did.

Before he went he asked whether there was anything else, anything particular that I would like to say. On the matter. I fetched Schopenhauer and made him copy out a few lines from *Art*: "The concept, the connection we perceive between abstractions and actual objects, is eternally barren in all art; the artist shows us the world's deepest meaning in a language that the intellect cannot comprehend, in the same way that a sleepwalker can give clear answers about things that he has no knowledge of when he is awake."

When evening came I brought the mattress down again and slept on the floor in the shop. It was only ordinary four-millimetre glass in the shop window and I had nothing more on the door than a simple mortice lock with a key on the inside.

The newspaper the next morning had the Madonna on the front page. And now she'd got her name. The local editor obviously couldn't manage to write about anything that didn't have a name. She was a masterpiece and worth millions of crowns. In the headline she was called "A Painting Worth a Million". The part that dealt with Dardel was lifted from an encyclopaedia. And every idiotic and banal thing that I'd said, and for that matter

Schopenhauer too, was also there. It was a good article. It was perhaps the best and truest piece that's been written about the Madonna. Triptych was correctly spelled. The photo covered two columns. It was embarrassing to see my round, self-satisfied and ridiculously bald head above hers that was upright, authentic and pure. In a box just beside it was the interview with Paula's mother. She knew everything about Paula's new music and her life in Stockholm and her enormous fortune but she wouldn't reveal any of it. A mother and daughter must be able to have their secrets. She waged an incessant battle to protect her own and Paula's private lives. On all fronts. Nothing weighs on you as much as secrets, she said. But she was really looking forward to seeing her own little Paula on the stage again. No, she wouldn't be going up to Stockholm. Yes, of course she was invited to the première. But she hated seeing her own picture in the newspapers. And those vulgar weekly magazines. She didn't dare, she didn't want to take any risks, a mother's heart can break as easily as a toy balloon.

At intervals throughout the day several of the neighbours called in. They stood and looked at the back of the painting. And we talked a little.

"It's really quite remarkable," they said.

"Yes," I said. "It's really quite remarkable."

After five o'clock the spectators started to arrive. They stood out on the pavement in the dusk looking at her. I don't think they talked to one another, their bodies swayed to and fro a little and they shaded their eyes with their hands to keep out the light from inside the window. Most of them stood there just for a few moments and then got in their cars and drove off again; none of them made time to come in to see me.

When it was completely dark I set up a little reflector lamp behind the curtain that divided the workshop from the shop and let it shine out through the window. Then when I put out the ceiling lights in the shop I could see them all very clearly, it looked as if they were all in an aquarium.

At seven o'clock Gulliver came. He pushed his way through and was almost pressing his face against the glass. He stood completely still, with only his eyes moving backwards and forwards as he scrutinised the three parts of the painting. He must have realised that I was standing inside watching him. But that didn't bother him. Or else he wanted me to watch him.

And I did. I don't know why, but I didn't dare let him out of my sight for an instant.

I also recognised a few of the others. Two district medical officers and the county veterinary inspector. The vicar. The Savings Bank manager and a primary-school teacher who'd once bought two paintings from me. And the local editor of the county newspaper. Perhaps he was just checking to see whether what he'd written had had an effect. He wanted to see his own article as if in a mirror.

Gulliver stayed the longest of all. By ten o'clock he was alone. But he stayed on another half hour; then he straightened up and turned round very quickly, as if someone had called him, lumbered over to his car and went off too.

That evening I fastened a piece of copper wire to her frame and brought the other end over to my bed on the floor and wound it round my left wrist before I went to sleep. I sleep soundly. If it's possible to know anything about your own sleep.

The telephone woke me at two o'clock in the morning. My immediate thought was: Something has happened to Paula. That thought has always been in the back of my mind. Although in fact nobody has ever known that I'm the one to be rung if anything happens to Paula. I quickly pulled off the copper wire and jumped up to answer it.

It was a journalist on one of the evening papers. Thank God, I said, or rather, shouted. He'd happened to see the county paper. Was I that picture-framer? How could I be sure that it was a Dardel? Was this the first time I'd speculated in art? How old was I? Would I sell it in Sweden or abroad? Why did I say "Thank God" when I answered the telephone? What other artists did I have in my collection? Tiredness gave me the patience to reply to all his questions in a calm and almost friendly manner.

Then I had to have half a glass of aquavit to get myself off to sleep again.

I F ANYONE ASKS me what happened in the next few days I can't tell them. People came, that's all I can remember. But I don't know in what order they came, in many cases I don't know what they wanted of me, I've forgotten their names, and I can't say what they looked like. I was tired and confused and elated. At night I tied the copper wire to the Madonna and slept for several hours. I ached in my whole body and had such vivid dreams that I might just as well have been awake. Four TV channels came and did reports on me and the Madonna. I was feverish: the sweat would suddenly start pouring off me even though I was shaking with cold. Yet I felt healthier and more wide awake and exhilarated than ever before. We were in all the newspapers, the Madonna and I.

The evening we appeared on the TV news programme, huge crowds of people came and just stood outside the shop looking in. They didn't want to see the Madonna, they wanted to see me. I went and stood by the window for a moment and showed myself.

Somewhere Schopenhauer said: "Life is never beautiful."

I thought life was preposterously beautiful.

Paula sent me flowers, those red and yellow tulips that Dardel used in *Visit to an Eccentric Lady*.

Museum and gallery curators started to turn up. They talked a lot about that period in Dardel's life. He'd lost the only woman he'd ever loved, he roamed around in Europe, drinking and painting the whole time, mostly drinking whisky. He had love affairs with men and women and probably with demons too in a random and giddy confusion: it was the most productive period in his life. Everyone was aware that he'd also painted a few things that had remained unknown. And all the experts were willing to provide certificates of authenticity.

"Yes, please," I said.

There is a brown envelope somewhere that contains seven hand-written certificates that *The Madonna with the Dagger* is with absolute certainty painted by Nils Dardel. Beyond all doubt. On the outside of the envelope are the figures 38×47. That's the size of that matchstick picture.

Peter Dahl came, the painter. He's the greatest living artist in Sweden. He remarked: "I think this painting says something about its own times that no one else knew. No one except Dardel." And he went on: "It's not done now to produce art that says something that not everyone already knows. We are the first people to know every-thing about their times." It wasn't particularly well put. But that was what he said. So it's probably true.

Many people came to take photographs. And we posed, the Madonna and I. We never took payment. It never occurred to us that we could get paid. I smiled on all the photographs, boastfully and idiotically. Many of the newspapers cut me out.

One of the photographers stayed for three days. Actually he wasn't a photographer, but I didn't know that then. He took his pic-tures on the first day, and then he just sat on a chair staring at her – I'd turned her in towards the room for the journalists' sake. He was stocky and bald and had short, stubby fingers and a goatee beard and glasses with heavy black rims. He was staying in Lundgren's guest-house by the bus station. We chatted to each other; he asked me, for example, how old I was.

"Thirty-one," I said. "But it feels as if I've got older over the last few days. Or bigger."

"As if you'd started growing again," he said. "Though you'll soon be middle-aged."

"Yes," I nodded.

"It's not you who've changed," he said. "It's your destiny that's grown."

"But finding a real masterpiece," I said. "That's pretty unusual."

"Anyone could have found her," he said. "The picture could have fallen to the floor so that the frame dropped open. Don't over-estimate yourself."

"But I was half prepared for it in a way," I said. "I've always kind of felt in myself that something was going to happen one day."

That was a lie, pure and simple.

"All of us feel in ourselves that something is going to happen to us," he said. "It's born in us."

I didn't ask anything, not his name nor what he did nor where he came from. He was probably some sort of journalist; perhaps he worked for a serious journal since he gave himself so much time and was so thoughtful and earnest.

"At the beginning I almost thought I was starting to go mad," I said. "Now what I feel most is a solemn, restrained pleasure."

"If she were hanging in the Museum of Modern Art she would seem more manageable," he said. "She's too grand and strong for this little village, she's as powerful as a hydrogen bomb."

He was the only one I really talked to. All the others just tried to question me, they wanted to know everything but gave themselves no time to listen when I explained things. And I remember that we talked about journalists, he and I. Journalists and newspapers and radio and TV. About the way a high, bright space is constructed, and beneath that space a landscape one thinks one recognises just because it is so unambiguously a landscape, but one in which nothing is true or unfalsified, and instead of real objects and living creatures and vegetation there are just words and concepts and fantasies. But you only notice it when you yourself are placed in that landscape. It was probably he who said that.

And it was he who sent a large and accurate colour photograph of the Madonna to Paula. Otherwise she had only seen her in the newspapers, since she couldn't come over. It was I who'd asked him to do it; I gave him the address. He'd never heard of her. She phoned immediately she received the picture, a couple of days later.

"I obviously didn't fully understand how fantastic she was," she said. "But I can see now."

"And yet that's just a photograph," I said.

57

"I've taped her up above my bed," said Paula. "As a reminder of everything. Of you and all the unbelievable things that are happening to us, and of the fact that we have some sort of responsibility for her."

"That's exactly what your mother would have done," I said.

"I'm sorry," said Paula.

"I think Dardel intended her to hang in a church," I said. "Up behind the altar."

"Yes," said Paula. "There probably are churches like that."

The art-dealers who came were easy to recognise. They looked as if they were in a hurry, they hardly even glanced at the Madonna, they just checked hastily to make sure there weren't any competitors there. Then they asked if they could speak to me alone. I took them into the workshop and pulled the curtain across behind us.

"Have you decided on a price?" the dealer would ask.

"I don't understand what you mean," I would say.

"You don't need to be embarrassed," the art-dealer would respond. "Just name the figure."

They all patronised me with equal arrogance. I was a cretin who'd happened to draw a winning ticket in a lottery.

"I'm actually intending to keep her," I said. "In my private collection."

A few of them asked, in some astonishment, what other masters I had in my collection. But most of them just said:

"When all's said and done, you must have put a price on her. In your heart of hearts. What's the price on your ticket?"

Some went on to add: "Don't give her to an auction firm, whatever you do. You'll only be cheated."

"No one will ever be able to cheat me," I said. "And she has no price."

"So you've thought of taking offers?" they asked.

"No. I haven't thought of asking for offers, either."

"But you don't mind if we name a figure? Just as a suggestion?"

58

"If you do that," I said, "I'd like a written offer. Signed and witnessed and valid for at least six months."

I received eight neatly written, signed and witnessed offers that week. I put them in the drawer under the telephone. Some simply rang. The managing director of one of the biggest forestry companies in northern Sweden rang late one evening, just wanting to say that he thought he could probably put up so and so many million. I'd seen him in *This Week*, and I knew what he looked like.

"But you haven't seen her," I said.

"I'm used to buying sight unseen," he said. "I buy millions of pines and spruces every year that I've never seen."

"I never thought of that," I said.

"I like to be surprised by art," he said. "A work of art should come like a thief in the night. Buying paintings that you already know inside out is meaningless, you could equally well paint them yourself."

"I promise I'll consider it," I said.

I took a note of his number. "You'll be hearing from me," I said. "If the day comes when I can't manage to keep her."

Early one morning there was a loud knocking at the door. I'd just undone the copper wire round my wrist and was standing with the rolled-up mattress under my arm. It was Gulliver.

"May I come in?" he asked.

"You're always welcome," I said.

I meant it – for days I'd had nothing but strangers around me, and I felt I'd known him for a long time.

"Are we alone?" he asked.

"Yes," I said. "We're alone."

"I've come with an offer," he said. "This time you won't escape. Everyone sooner or later gets to the point where it's no longer worth trying to resist."

"I haven't asked for any offers," I said.

"We've formed a consortium," he said. "A few colleagues in the field and myself. We wouldn't have done that if you hadn't been open to offers. That's a prerequisite, as it were."

"I've had a few other offers too," I said. "I've put them in a drawer."

"Well," he said. "So you don't even read them."

"I'm going to keep them," I said. "They belong together with the Madonna in some way."

"But this is one you must read," he said. He took his wallet from his back pocket, opened it, and drew out a small folded piece of paper.

"I think," he said, "that this will break through the final barrier for you. Even if it doesn't do so for us."

I leaned the mattress against a stack of oil paintings. As I opened out the slip of paper he went on: "He was a devil, that Dardel. This is the biggest transaction in my life." And for a moment his flabby lower lip quivered with a kind of emotion.

When I read the amount I felt my hands jerk as if they wanted to tear the paper to pieces straight away. I understood what he meant by the words "the final barrier". The absurdity of the ridiculously high figure hit me like a fist in the face.

"Those times are past," I said. "The time when you could earn big money from art. That was a few years ago. Now it's overseas property."

"To hell with that," said Gulliver. "Our view in the consortium was that she's perfect – they said that on TV – and if something's perfect, there's no risk."

"Everything that's real," I said, "is perfect. Nothing can be other than it is."

I also managed to say: "But I'll put it in the drawer with the other offers."

Then I asked him to leave. "I must get dressed," I said. "Customers may start arriving at any moment."

I actually sold a lot of oil paintings in gold frames for quite a few days. It was as if some kind of infection had been transferred from the Madonna to the genuine hand-painted landscapes, as if they had become more real and more desirable because of her proximity.

In the doorway Gulliver turned and said: "I could see that it was pretty close to the mark. It showed in your face. In the end you'll realise that you haven't got any choice."

I ought to mention here what sort of landscape they saw, the people who came to visit the Madonna and me. Because they saw the landscape too. If they came in the mornings the lake was hidden in the mist. The village began where the mist stopped. And beyond the last buildings, the three-storey flats built by the council in the sixties, the fields continued. The agricultural landscape stretched right to the low horizon where the forests started. Some people called the forests "mountains". But they weren't mountains, it was just the end of the clay plains and the beginning of a moraine. The mist disappeared at midday and then you could really see nothing but sky. Though sometimes there would still be a line of haze over the river, like a thin wisp of smoke curling into the distance without actually ending anywhere. Apart from the sky you were also aware of the oak, ash and lime trees in people's gardens. When they all left again, those who'd come to see the Madonna, they had to drive ten miles through the mist to get back out to the main road.

On one of the very first days someone asked me how I'd got her insured.

"I sleep with her at night," I replied. "And I tie a copper wire from the frame to my wrist."

But I could immediately hear for myself how inadequate and pitiful that sounded, and what a childish concept it was. So I rang the insurance company where we'd always had the business insured. Fittings, fixtures and stock: fifty thousand crowns.

It wasn't as simple as I'd imagined. I would need a burglar alarm. And I would have to give the precise value of the Madonna. I stated the amount that was written in the offer from Gulliver, and my tongue stumbled over the figures. I asked whether the insurance company could help me with the burglar alarm. And what the whole thing would cost.

A man came from the insurance company that same afternoon. He looked round for a few moments and then said: "Two thousand crowns for the burglar alarm and eleven thousand for the insurance."

"I haven't got that sort of money," I said.

"You're the richest man in the district. With this picture."

"I've got nothing except the Madonna," I replied.

"Liquid assets," he said, "that's no problem. I can help you. For the time being. The only difficulty with money is how to invest it."

"Thank you," I said, "but I'd rather try to manage for myself."

Before he went he said: "But all these other paintings. They must be worth hundreds of thousands."

"They're completely worthless," I replied. "The frames are more expensive than the paintings themselves."

"What would you take for that one?" he asked, pointing to a clump of trees and a little lake with four white birds swimming on it. "Shall we say eight thousand?"

"It costs four hundred," I said. "Six hundred for the big ones and four hundred for the smaller ones. There are seven birds on the big ones." I rubbed my bald scalp with the palm of my hand. I always do that when I feel confused but at the same time completely certain of something.

"No," he said. "You're trying to cheat me. The devil himself would have a hard time doing business with you."

"If you could pay eight thousand," I asked, "you'd buy it?"

"Right away," he replied. "On the nail."

I borrowed the money from the Savings Bank. I asked for fifteen thousand, but they pressed twenty thousand on me. "We're pleased to be able to give you a helping hand," said the assistant manager. "That's what we're here for. You're always welcome, you know that. In your case we could extend it an awful lot more."

A few years before, when I wanted to buy the delivery van, they only let me borrow ten thousand, although I needed seventeen thousand. I had to arrange the rest on hire purchase.

I never understood the burglar alarm. If anyone touched the painting or broke the window or pushed on the door when it was locked or walked through the shop after the ceiling lights were off, a siren blew that sounded like an air-raid warning. But I could turn the whole thing off with a switch behind the curtain.

That Saturday it was time for the New Paula.

She'd been in the newspapers every day. No, not her, that was the old one, the former Paula who had laughed and pouted her lips for the photographs, the girl with the golden angel hair, the most successful and most enviable child of our times. There wasn't a single photograph from recent years; the journalists and photographers hadn't even been allowed to come to the rehearsals of the last few weeks.

By eight in the morning I was finally alone. The last visitors had gone, an editor from Gothenburg and the farmer from the yellow house who'd come to fetch the matchstick picture. I switched on the burglar alarm before I went upstairs and sat down in front of the TV. I was happy and expectant, but at the same time my fear sent a taste of blood to my mouth, as if it were I and not she who was being forced out on to the stage to be unveiled and exposed, to be both magnificent and helpless. For safety's sake and in order to be ready for anything, I drank half a glass of aquavit.

I asked Paula the other day how she would describe her life. She replied with these lines that she'd scribbled down on the yellow wrapping paper from a bottle of Veuve Clicquot:

Soprano. Artiste of the year in eleven different newspapers. Three times in five of them. Twice a prizewinner in the Swedish Music Festival. Artiste's award from the trades union movement – five thousand crowns. Audience records at fourteen open-air concerts. Seventeen gold discs. Five platinum discs. *Litteris et artibus* medal – presented by the King. Six Grammy awards for the best singing artiste. Etc.

She wrote that in her own hand.

MANY THINGS in contemporary life have had a deep appeal for me, but not music. Not serious electronic music, nor rap or ska or funk or soul or house or heavy metal or trash metal or new wave or speed metal or hip-hop or bat-cave. I've obviously not been completely untouched or my left hand wouldn't be able to rattle off all those names so easily, but I've never been sucked into the music and become one with it, not as I have with Bruckner's Symphony in D-minor or Honegger's Oratorios. Well, just once I thought to myself: This concerns me, someone has created this music for me; and that was when I heard "The Unforgettable Fire" by U2 for the first time. It was Maria who gave me that, the woman who lived with me for a few months. But when I played the record again the feeling had gone; it must have just been the situation that made me feel emotional: Maria in her deliberate self-abandonment wanting to give me the best things she knew.

Paula must have felt more or less the same. Of course she's lived constantly with the new music, but what's helped her to feel at ease with it is everything in it that sounded old and well-known and remote in time, everything that alluded to the kind of beauty that my grandfather built his pianos for. Paula isn't a modern person. A modern person has no energy to love any other time than his own. Paula's time is the nineteenth century, her music that of the Romantics and the early Impressionists.

This was what I was thinking as I sat down in front of the TV. And I went on thinking about it as I watched and listened to Paula.

It was ghastly. I wanted to run away. I could have smashed the television set. I was shaking and trembling with shame and embarrassment. And I remember that I was kneading my scalp with both

65

hands the whole time as if I'd got frostbite inside my head and was having to rub my brain warm again. For a moment I also felt that I should rush over to her mother and stop her seeing this dreadful thing, it must be abominable for her to see Paula so degraded and humiliated – no, to see her degrading and humiliating herself.

My jeans and shirt were dripping with sweat afterwards; I had to undress and take a shower and let the water flow over me for what must have been an hour.

I don't need to describe the music or the amazingly lithe and self-assured, not to say acrobatic, dancing. Everyone has seen Paula and heard her. Everyone can see her on video whenever they want. The clinging leather dress with different shades of colour actually hinting at an absence of clothes, a false nakedness; jewellery hanging and swinging from her neck and wrists and ankles and over her breasts, those baubles that in close-up revealed themselves as coins, dollars and pounds and marks and crowns; her face made up to look like an even more childlike little girl's face than her previous one, one that everybody could recognise by the great big startled eyes and pouting mouth. And her sleek indigo hair shaped to follow the curve of her cheeks and ending in small plaits with glittering coins at the tips. I couldn't recognise her and yet it was her without a doubt, her voice and movements and hands and eyes that seemed to be saying: There's not a single person more innocent and defence-less than I, I can't help myself, I'm just a little baby that somebody has to look after.

A critic wrote afterwards in one of the evening papers what were probably the truest words to have been written about the new Paula, this other Paula: "Hell's bells and come in your trousers! A saucier and sexier show and a randier singer have never before been seen in the Kingdom of Sweden! And never have we heard music that's been so absolutely right! Like the acid rock of the past but with an incessant raga as background resonance, as if someone were making love with a sitar or a drum the whole time in the hollow space beneath the stage. I can't help it – it has to be said: I had an erection from the first note to the last!"

66

The headline was GIRL-CHILD WHO BECAME A SHE-DEVIL.

The national daily *Dagens Nyheter* said: "Somebody has to give voice to the dreadful, unbearable pain of our times. Perhaps Paula is the one to do it."

Just as I came out of the shower there was a ring at the back door. I wrapped the bath-towel round me and went down and opened the door. It was Paula's mother. Her face was burning red and streaked with excitement and mascara and rouge.

"Haven't you been watching Paula?" she screeched.

"Yes," I replied. "And then I had to go and have a shower."

"I'm so wonderfully happy," she said. "I'm crying."

"I can see that," I said.

"You feel so ecstatic and ready to burst that you simply have to talk to somebody," she said. "To anybody."

"Come in," I said. "I'll just put some clothes on."

"I actually came for a reason," she said. "I wondered if you had a bottle of champagne."

"I'm afraid I haven't."

"We ought to celebrate this," she said.

"Yes," I said. "Paula was marvellous."

"And I thought you'd have bought some drink in," she said. "Because of this amazing painting."

"I've got a half-bottle of aquavit," I replied. "That's all."

"It's not the same as champagne," said Paula's mother. "But *faute de mieux . . .*"

I brought the bottle and gave it to her. Then we said goodnight and she went home.

At one o'clock that night Paula rang. I'd already gone to bed.

"It's the middle of the night," I said. "I'm trying to sleep."

"I'm sorry," said Paula. "I didn't think of that."

I could hear a crowd of people laughing and shouting all around her, trying to outdo a loudspeaker system that was playing one of her new songs.

"Where are you?" I asked.

"At Uncle Erland's," she replied. "Just a little party. For me."

"You ought to sleep too," I said. "It's over now. You shouldn't do too much."

Then she said: "How was I?"

That was the question she'd really phoned to ask.

"You were fantastic," I responded. "Absolutely fantastic."

"Is that the truth?"

"I would never be able to lie to you," I said. "I can't lie at all."

We blew to one another and said goodnight. It was almost impossible to speak above the noise around her: Paula had to whistle instead of blowing.

I sat down and listened to Mahler. That was what I needed right then. Mahler used to read Dostoevsky when he thought that life was almost unbearable. Misery and lawlessness and suffering and the capriciousness of life provided him with some kind of comfort.

Hermann Prey was singing. I listened over and over again to one of the songs until I could finally write it down.

Then I sat all day Sunday trying to translate it. It was much harder than I first thought. *"Ich bin der Welt abhanden gekommen."*

"I AM LOST TO THE WORLD."

It wasn't exactly a brilliant translation, but it did quite feel as if I'd managed to make some of Mahler's melancholy my own. I don't know whether any serious translator has bothered himself with this particular song.

On Monday morning I hung a sign on the door: CLOSED. ILLNESS.

Then I went over to Paula's mother.

She didn't open the door, but she called from the hallway.

"Who is it? It's not nine o'clock yet."

"It's only me," I said. "You're not ill, are you?"

She unlocked the door and let me in.

"That aquavit was strong," she said. "I haven't properly recovered yet."

She had her dressing gown on and her face wasn't made up. It was the first time I'd seen her like that. She had a bruise under one eye. She was a frightful sight.

"I fell out of bed," she said, covering the bruise with her fingers. "But I feel a lot better now, anyway."

"I need Crackshot's telephone number," I said.

"It's ex-Directory," she replied. "In those circles people have to have an ex-Directory number."

"That's why I have to get it from you," I said. "Directory Enquiries won't give it."

"I'm going to get an ex-Directory number myself," she said. "Then I can give it to close friends. Instead of boxes of chocolates and things."

"I could ask Paula," I said. "But I'd rather not disturb her."

"Have you got Paula's number?" she asked.

"Yes," I said. "Of course I have."

"You ought to have an ex-Directory number too," said Paula's mother. "With your painting and everything."

"I'm not that sort of person," I said.

"His real name is Erland," she said.

"I know," I replied. "But everyone calls him Crackshot."

"What do you want him for?"

"I just thought I'd get in touch with him," I said. "Not for any particular reason."

"He's wonderful," she said. "All that he's done for her. She means the world to him."

"Yes," I said. "Almost."

"So obviously he might deserve some flowers too. That was what you thought."

"Yes," I said. "I thought something like that. I'm glad that you reminded me of it."

"He likes orchids," she said. "The sort they have in transparent plastic boxes."

"I'll remember that," I said.

"It's funny you have to have the phone number to be able to send flowers," she said.

"Yes," I said. "It's funny."

Then she actually gave me the number.

"I think you should go back to bed," I said. "You can put a note on the door."

"Nonsense," she said. "I'm fine now. I'm glad you looked in. I've never felt better or happier in my whole life."

By the newspaper kiosk outside the bus station the previous day's placards were still on display, slightly fuzzy with frost. SUCCESS, I could see, and PAULA and BOMB.

I went into the florist's shop by the church and sent five white lilies to Paula. "And what shall we write on the card?" asked the assistant. I still had Mahler in my head, so I couldn't think of anything except "The beautiful trumpets are playing," and then just

70

my name. It struck me afterwards that perhaps white lilies were completely wrong.

When the assistant manager at the bank heard my business, he asked me to go in to the manager with him. We said good morning and he pointed to an armchair for me to sit in. It was hard to know how to express myself; I tried to think of the art-dealers I'd met recently. Yet I could still hear my voice getting shrill and breaking when I said: "I need some money. How much could I borrow against the Madonna?"

The bank manager laughed, but even his laugh was slightly squeaky and tense. "We're not pawnbrokers," he said.

"She's more secure than a thousand acres of farmland," I said. "Or an apartment block, or a forest, or a sawmill."

"That may be so," he replied. "But houses and businesses and land are different: they're solid, so to speak."

"She weighs more than thirty pounds," I said. "She's more substantial than any other object I know."

"It's not usual," he said. "We have our procedures. And unwritten rules. We're tied hand and foot."

"You've seen her," I said.

"Yes," he said. "I've seen her."

He was silent for some time.

"But we know you, of course," he said. "Everyone knows you. You don't need to put forward any security. A personal loan. No security and no guarantees. It's simply a matter of trust."

"Then it will all be wrong," I said. "My idea is that the Madonna should play exactly this role in my life."

I could hear myself how strange that sounded.

"And how would we be able to put a value on her?" the manager asked. "Our valuers only understand agricultural land and forest. Can't you simply turn her into cash?"

"No. I'll never sell her."

"You're all the same, you people who are really successful, you who get on best. You're as stubborn as hell. You never give an inch. That's something I've learned."

71

"I have written offers," I said. "They'd serve as well as any valuation."

And I handed him the little bundle, with Gulliver's offer at the bottom.

He looked through them long and carefully. At the end he couldn't help reading aloud.

"Fifteen million," he said. "Fifteen million."

"Yes," I said. "Fifteen million."

"I'll have to talk to Head Office," he said. "I'll do it for your sake. Can you come back tomorrow?"

"No," I said. "I'll wait."

He went out and was gone for almost half an hour. I tried to read a leaflet that was lying on his desk, called "Money". "There are people who really are significant in their own right," it said in an interview with the President of the Council of Europe.

When the bank manager came back, he said: "Well, in fact it's not beyond the bounds of possibility. In your case. What would you use the money for?"

"An investment," I replied. "A fantastic investment."

"She would have to stay here with us, in the vaults," he said. "From the point of view of security she's most comparable to gold ingots, according to Head Office. Purely a formality. She would remain your property, of course. And you could come to see her whenever you wanted."

"That won't be necessary," I replied. "I know her by heart. I could close my eyes and count the brush strokes and pigments."

Then he tried to get me to state the sum I needed. But I didn't know, I hadn't given a moment's thought to actual figures. He coaxed and cajoled, and we hummed and hawed, he went over to the window and stared out at the church, I picked up a piece of paper and a pen and pretended to write down some figures – I wrote out the alphabet from A to Z. But in the end he said: "Three million. Would three million be enough?"

I replied that that would probably be fine, it might even be more than was needed, but it was good not to have to worry any more. To be able to make good business deals you have to feel a sense of security and some kind of inner peace, I said.

We would be in touch, we agreed. When the time came.

We'd already taken leave of each other when he said: "I hope you don't feel as if you've insulted the Madonna. That you've degraded the work of art."

"It's not possible to degrade a work of art," I responded. "Dardel would have done the same himself."

And I paused on the threshold and quoted Schopenhauer: "Art is not matter but only form. A world of spirits."

Crackshot had a telephone-answering machine, of course. I rang ten times and repeated my telephone number. And what I wanted. For as long as I could manage to keep saying it.

He rang at three o'clock; I was sitting at the table in the framing workshop and working on a game of patience called Demon. If four spades hadn't ended up in the same pile I could have got it out.

"You needn't tell me who you are," he said. "I know. Paula often talks about you."

But I said anyway: "I'm the one who owns *The Madonna with the Dagger*. By Dardel."

"Yes," he said. "I know. Congratulations."

"Actually, Paula is joint owner," I said. "We both own it together. The two of us."

"She must have forgotten that," he said. "She's never said anything."

"In a way that makes the Madonna even more valuable for me," I said. "That's the way I am. I never bother about money."

"I have to be at the Stock Exchange in half an hour," he said. "The pub, that is. The Exchange. I've got an awful lot on."

"I can imagine," I said.

"So if there was anything you wanted from me," he said, "we could perhaps sort it out straight away."

"I want to buy Paula back," I said.

"Back?"

"Yes, back."

I didn't think that he would understand what I meant, I'd imagined that he would be absolutely speechless. But he wasn't.

"Well, well," he said. "And what do you want her for?"

"I want her to sing Schubert and Mendelssohn," I said. "And Ravel and Mahler. To play Satie and Grieg and Busoni."

I don't know why I mentioned Busoni.

"Is that all?" Crackshot asked.

"I want her to live with dignity, a completely authentic life," I said. "And develop. I know of no other person as talented as she is. So magnificent and so precious."

"I can agree with you there," he said. "She's a little pearl."

"Three million," I said. "I thought of offering you three million."

Even that didn't silence him.

"Do you realise," he said, "that it was I who created Paula? Without me she would be nothing."

"No," I replied, "I was the one who created her. I looked after her almost from the moment she was born."

"I see," he said.

"Of course, she had her parents," I went on, "but she was my child. We grew up together. She was my sister. I taught her everything."

"Aren't you more than ten years older than she is?"

"Yes," I said, "about that."

"Then you couldn't have grown up together, for God's sake."

"I didn't bother myself about those ten years," I said. "I made myself small again so that we could grow up together. I've never regretted it."

"You ought to be in a circus," said Crackshot. "The man who makes himself small when he feels like it."

"Your sneers don't bother me," I said. "You don't understand the situation. You don't know anything about Paula and me."

"She's not for sale," he said. "I'll never sell her."

He went on to explain to me what a childish fool I was, what a

74

laughable nonentity, what a small-time country bumpkin. "You've got stuck at puberty," he said. He wanted to give me a word of advice: I shouldn't kid myself that this painting worth millions had added an inch to my stature or made me one jot more remarkable, I was still a shitty little picture-frame maker, and if I ever tried to raise my eyes from my bench I'd collapse with dizziness and terror. I'd do best to hang on tight with both hands to my mitre-saw and glue and set-square.

Every word he said was true.

And then he started laughing, a great rumbling, thundering roar of a laugh, it sounded as if he was shouting and bawling at me and I had to hold the telephone receiver away from my ear to stop it hurting too much.

I wished he'd laughed at me like that and forced me into silence right at the beginning, before I'd said anything at all.

In the end we agreed: "We won't mention any of this to Paula."

"No," I said. "We won't do that."

Afterwards I lay down full length on the floor; I do that sometimes. There's nowhere safer to lie than on a floor. I might have fallen asleep for a moment, I don't remember. But after a while, a quarter of an hour or an hour, I got up and went out into the shop, turned off the burglar alarm and unlocked the door. I took down the sign that said CLOSED, ILLNESS. It really felt as if I'd suddenly become completely well again.

I regretted it afterwards. I could have played patience. I could have done anything at all. But at least I could have refrained from opening the shop that afternoon.

A customer came. I thought he was a customer, anyway.

He walked around the shop looking at the paintings one after another, and he lifted the curtain carefully and looked into the work-shop. He was wearing a thick blue overcoat with a belt; he was about my own age and had thick black hair combed in an S-shape down over his forehead. Now and again he stopped and scratched his chin with his right index finger, as if the genuine oil paintings had made him hesitant or uncertain.

"The little ones cost four hundred crowns," I said. "And the big ones six hundred."

"I don't usually understand art," he said, "but you've got a number of paintings here that are really quite fascinating and absorbing."

"It's never possible to be completely indifferent," I responded. "You can agonise till you get cramp in every muscle, but you can't manage to be totally indifferent."

He looked up and stared at me then, long and hard as if I too were a painting of something more serious and more meaningful than one might think at first. I rubbed my bald pate.

"Everything is constantly in motion and always recurs," he said. "It's never possible to escape."

That was a quotation, I recognised it. But I couldn't remember who had said it and I still don't know. It might have been Nietzsche.

Then he explained who he was. He said: "I should have introduced myself."

"It's not necessary," I replied. "Most of my customers remain anonymous to me. You can't get interested in every single person."

He was from the Inland Revenue. The local tax office. I think he called himself chief investigator.

"I see. I might have guessed," I said. "When I saw the way you were looking at the paintings."

"Fantastic business you've been doing lately," he said. "Huge sums in turnover. I must say it's seldom we hear of money like that in our little office. And we never see it in writing."

"Yes," I said. "I can scarcely comprehend it myself. I sometimes wake up in the middle of the night and have to come down here and put on the light to reassure myself that it's true. Though for me it has nothing at all to do with money."

"Really? If it's not a matter of money, then, what would you say it's actually about?"

"Art and money," I said, "are two completely different worlds.

Art is not concerned with markets. Not even the dirtiest money can soil a real work of art. Art is always completely pure and innocent.

"Everything that's genuine is innocent," I added.

"That sounded almost like a quotation from a book," he said.

"Yes," I replied, "it was."

"What dirty money were you talking about?"

"Any dirty money," I said. "It was part of the quotation."

"But you're running a business," he said, raising his arms and pointing round the walls. "This is a source of income. A firm."

"You have to support yourself somehow," I said. "I do what I can. And I hardly ever eat anything but porridge and milk."

I said all this even though I wasn't at all sure it was really anything to do with him.

"We've wondered a lot about your affairs," he said. "Recently. At the tax office. We can't make it all fit, however hard we try."

"You don't need to worry about me," I said. "I always get by."

"These enormous sums," he said. "Where do they come from? We read the newspapers, you know."

"Yes," I said. "I'm inclined to think that everything is pure invention. I try to avoid reading the papers."

"So that's why I'm here," he said. "We would like to know a little more. We would like you to explain the whole story to us."

"It's not really very strange or remarkable," I said.

And then I gave a simple account of everything that I've written in these 77 pages, from my great-grandfather in Raggsjö and the auctions for the mission, right up to this man himself and this very afternoon when he walked into the shop and I thought he was a normal customer. I took him up to the flat and showed him the black chest and helped him to read Great-Grandfather's ornate lettering, PRAISED BE THE LORD, and I let him try Grandfather's piano so that he could smell the delightful aroma of cherry-tree and pear-tree wood, and I brought out old papers and pointed out specific lines or phrases that might be of interest to him, my grandfather's unintelligible designs and grandmother's account books and receipts for all the sugar and yeast my father had bought, and my

77

examination certificates and my mother's death certificate. I let him sit in the armchair in front of the bookshelves, while I myself stood in the middle of the floor as I talked; I enjoyed having an audience, it felt good to be able to tell my story at such length and in such detail. I made expansive gestures and imitated voices and demonstrated the way various people had walked or moved, and he listened attentively. I played my mandolin to him, *"O Sole Mio"*. I liked him. He laughed openly and sincerely at our puppets, Paula's and mine.

When I finally stopped, with the words "And here we are now, you and I," he said:

"None of that sounds particularly credible."

He rubbed his chin with his whole hand, almost as if he was suffering some inexplicable pain, and repeated it:

"No, no sensible person would believe a word of all that. It smacks of forgery and deception throughout."

"That's depressing," I replied. "I really have done my best."

And I had. I couldn't do any better.

"But at the same time you're so damned honest," he said. "So decent that I almost feel sorry for you."

"Yes," I said.

"Everything you say is obviously true," he said. "But as a government body we can hardly place any faith in it. We must test its reliability."

"I'm not very good at talking," I said. "But if I'd written it all down so that you could examine it word for word, you'd have believed me."

He rubbed his chin even harder and was silent for a long time. Then he spoke again:

"What you said sounded fine. Crystal clear. We'll have to think about it. I'll test it on my colleagues. I think it will hold up. Please don't bother to put it all on paper."

"I hardly ever write anything down," I said. "I mentioned that I translated one of Mahler's songs yesterday, but otherwise I never write."

He wouldn't let me offer him anything. But I didn't have anything to offer anyway.

"If I can afford it one day," he said as he left, "I might buy a painting from you."

Paula rang that night. She always telephoned after performances. We said the things we usually said. And then she told me that Uncle Erland had got her a bodyguard now. He would go everywhere with her by day, and at night he would sleep in the hall. A madman had rung up and wanted to buy her. He'd offered several million crowns. And you can never be sure with fools like that. So, for safety's sake.

"I'm terribly worried about you as well," I said. "So we should be very grateful."

And I told her about the man from the tax office coming and how easily I'd sorted things out with him.

I F YOU DIG in quicklime under an apple tree when you plant it and keep on burning big fires right by it, it will grow and blossom and produce fruit within a few weeks. I don't know whether that's true.

For a month or so it felt as if life had suddenly put me in an artificial, not to say unnatural, heat. I sweated, my cheeks were flushed, my fingertips tingled and burned as if I'd held them over a candle flame. And I actually imagined that I was growing, that I was becoming grander and more significant and more flourishing.

Admittedly the journalists and art dealers had stopped coming, and the inquisitive people pretending to be customers had also become fewer, but the Madonna was still there with me, incandescent and radiant. And everything that was happening to Paula helped to raise the temperature of my existence.

Paula's mother had once again started buying all the weekly magazines she could get hold of, and I borrowed them all when she'd read them. She brought new ones every day and took away the old ones. I sat in the shop reading, with half an eye on the magazine and half on the Madonna, so to speak, and without my thinking about it or understanding it, a sort of mysterious connection grew up between the two, Paula and the Madonna. Paula was in every issue, often on the cover and always inside the magazine. There were articles about clothes and eating habits, her income and the make-up she used, her childhood and the singing teacher she went to every day, and the big secrets in her life. One magazine announced a competition called "Find Paula's Father". "That extremely, not to say pathologically, musical immigrant who disappeared so inexplicably when she was only five," they wrote. "We will pay twenty thousand crowns to anyone who finds him." Almost everything in those magazines was new to me, and I often managed to read several pages in a row with genuine curiosity, as if I didn't know her.

I needn't really describe all this, since most people will recall quite clearly what was written about her in magazines and newspapers.

The greatest amount of space was devoted to her love affairs. She often seemed to have three men at the same time: other artistes and singers, film directors, millionaires, a Belgian count, a couple of TV newsreaders, a tennis player, a lawyer and several others, I can't remember them all. Paula and I never spoke about such things – it had nothing to do with us.

I sometimes missed the many visitors who had come to see the Madonna and me at the beginning. It was strangely empty in the shop and workshop. I'd thought that a masterpiece like her would retain its attraction for ever, that she would never lose her power. Occasionally I would take a little drink of aquavit or a couple of aspirin in the afternoons to assuage the fever and anxiety and divert my thoughts from all the strangers I was expecting but who never came.

I mentioned it to Paula. "It feels as if almost anything might happen," I said.

"Everything is a matter of chance," she said. "That's something I've always known."

"I've never thought about it before," I replied.

Then I hardly thought about anything else except chance for several days.

Chance is an evil and loathsome power; it's best to put as little trust in it as possible. But it's generous, and there's no other force or authority that states so clearly that everything we receive is given to us by grace and favour, that everything is undeserved, and thus we can also hope to receive much more in the future. The only thing chance demands is that we should be humble. If you want to defend yourself against chance, if you don't want to be subject to it or don't want anything particular from it, then your only recourse is to try to hide somewhere where chance will never pursue you.

But there's no certainty that that will be any good. It's possible that we carry chance with us wherever we go, that we have it inside us. There's something in us that has more sense than our own intelligence. Perhaps that is chance.

Two letters came that I hadn't been expecting. They seemed to confirm what I'd been saying, that almost anything could happen.

One was from Maria, the woman who had been staying with me for a couple of months. We had really been cohabiting and she had never actually moved out. She had just gone travelling around a little, that's all. At the moment, she was staying with a friend in Gävle. She would soon be coming home again. I was not to forget that she owned half of that marvellous painting. But she knew me so well, and she was convinced in her heart of hearts that I hadn't for an instant thought of cheating her. She was so happy for us. Hugs and kisses. She just wanted to mention a paragraph in the law about the joint home of a cohabiting couple. And I was to look after myself and the painting till she came, it might be another month or so, but that didn't matter, time has no significance when people really love one another.

The second letter was from a Dieter Goldmann in Karlstad. He told me the history of the Madonna. I'd never believed I would ever find out where she came from. I'd realised that she'd had an existence before she became mine, of course, and sometimes I'd even amused myself by trying to invent a life story for her, but I'd avoided becoming too personal or indiscreet. There was an aura of sublimity and discretion surrounding her. But Dieter Goldmann knew everything. His letter was a gift that chance wanted to present to me. If I feel like it I'll say what this letter contained later on. In the last few lines he pointed out that she thus uncontestably belonged to him; his rights of ownership could in no way be called into question; he would call in and fetch her some time in the spring. He worked in insurance, and would always be able to find a reason for a business trip.

That evening I moved the mattress back down to the shop again. And that night I dreamed that the Madonna stepped out of the frame and came over to me and crept under the blanket and said that she was mine for ever.

Paula rang in the last few days before Christmas and told me she'd moved. It was Uncle Erland's Christmas present to her, a three-room apartment on Karlaplan in Stockholm. It had been bought by Paula Music Ltd. She hadn't known anything about it, the bodyguard who was driving her home after the performance had just driven her there, and all her furniture and clothes and odds and ends were already in place. "Now you can come and stay with me whenever you want," Paula said. "And the bodyguard has got his own room, too."

That Christmas we sent each other presents, Paula and I – something we'd never done before. Either we thought that we could afford them at last or that only now did we need to. I wrote out the translation of the Mahler song on a sheet of water-colour paper and framed and glazed it. It looked very pretty. And from Paula I got *The Guinness Book of Records*. The most silent place on earth is a laboratory called The Dead Room in New Jersey, where absolutely nothing can be heard. The highest body temperature a human being has ever survived is 46.5° centigrade, and that was Willie Jones, a 52-year-old negro in Atlanta, Georgia.

THERE ARE FAR too many of us. If I had just wanted to put a story together to amuse myself and maybe Paula, I would have made us three or four characters, no more. I could have well done without my ancestors and Paula's parents and Crackshot and the bodyguard and Gulliver and Dieter Goldmann and several others. I would like to have written a simpler and more manageable account. Time and time again I get cramp in this little bulbous muscle between the index finger and thumb on my left hand. And here comes yet another character.

She turned up when I reopened the shop after the Christmas break. I started talking about what the landscape paintings cost, but she wasn't interested; she immediately climbed into the window and squatted there looking at the Madonna. She was small and round and her hair was blond and frizzy. She stayed sitting there so long without moving that when she finally tried to rise her leg had gone numb, and I had to lift her down on to the floor and help her to stand upright. Since Maria left me I'd hardly touched a woman; it was lovely to hold her for those few seconds.

When I let go of her, she said:

"Once you've found Dardel, you can never forsake him. That passion for the problems of form. That artistic discipline. And aristocratic virtuosity. He had immersed himself in a deeper suffering than other people."

"Yes," I said. "That's probably true."

"I'm a Dardelian," she said.

"Dardelian?"

"In the same way that others might be Nietzscheans or Wagnerians or Wittgensteinians," she explained.

84

"In that case," I said, "I'm a Dardelian too."

"Just imagine," she said, "being ill enough for such sensuality. Although ill is probably the wrong word – there was just a fundamental incurability in his character. He had no choice, he had to be ambitious and challenging, as if driven by an incessant ache in his brain. It's the poisonous aspect of him that I love, the part that acts like a drug or an intoxicant. The dangerous and the unnerving and the morbid."

"I think I understand what you mean," I said.

"He was so foreign," she went on, "he would have been a foreigner wherever he'd been born or lived. As a Swede he was a mistake."

"You're an art historian," I said.

"I read history of art at university," she said, running her fingers through her hair and making it even more ruffled and bouffant. "I wrote my thesis on Surrealism in Sweden."

"Good God," I said. "Is that you? *Dreams Beneath an Arctic Sky*? I've got it."

"Yes," she said. "That's me."

I fetched the chair from my desk and asked her to sit down. It was the first time I'd met anyone who'd written a book on art, one that I had on my shelves. She looked a little surprised, but she sat down.

"With Mörner's *Close to the Sea* on the cover," I said.

"That's the one," she said. "A fantastic painting."

"And what museum are you working at now?" I asked.

"I'm working at the local tax office," she replied. "There are no jobs for art historians."

I didn't believe her; I tried a careful smile. She smiled too from time to time, a smile that seemed to erase everything we'd said so far, so that we had to start again from the beginning.

"But you liked the Madonna," I said.

"I'd venture to suggest," she said, "that she is his most significant work."

"The tax people have already been here," I said. "A chap with his hair combed in an S-shape over his forehead."

"That's right," she replied. "I'm his boss. We weren't at all satisfied with his report."

She went on to explain to me that my tax declarations had been unsatisfactory every year, but that they'd tempered justice with mercy because the sums involved were so ridiculously small. My declaration of just two sums, one for outgoings and one for income, was actually not permissible, and now they realised of course that the extent of my business would necessitate an extremely thorough investigation and audit. She also mentioned some of the many laws and statutes that I as a businessman had to comply with.

"When you talk about things like that," I said, "it's almost imposible to believe that you're an art historian."

"Art historians are parasites," she said, smiling her peculiar smile, "they produce nothing but dung. They have no fundamental connection to reality."

"But what about you yourself?"

"That was a long time ago," she replied. "I knew no better then. I was blinded by all that superficial spirituality and beauty."

"You said you were a Dardelian."

"That was a regression. I was taken by surprise and got a bit flustered. I'm feeling fine again now."

Then she wanted to examine my book-keeping.

I fetched the drawer where I put all the receipts and bits of paper.

"When I make my tax declaration," I said, "I sort them out. Payments in one pile and income in another. That's all there is to it."

I was rather proud of that drawer, it really contained everything. No book-keeping in the world could be more complete. I pulled it out and showed her a little piece of cardboard on which was written: "Received ten marigolds for the shop window from PM."

"Who is PM?" she asked.

"Paula's mother. She has the music shop on the other side of the street."

"I don't like your making fun of me," she said. "You obviously haven't realised that this is serious. You're trying to inflate your humility into pathos. Marigolds!"

86

"I'm doing my best," I said. "As I've always done."

"That's what they all say. Everyone who owes tax comes out with the same excuse: 'I did my best.' We get rather tired of hearing it in the tax office."

I put the drawer back under the counter again.

"Wouldn't you like to look at the Madonna a little more?" I asked. "I can lift her down on to the floor for you."

But she merely made an impatient gesture with her hand towards the Madonna, glanced at the clock and got up, saying: "If we can get some help we can probably sort all this out. It's not you personally we're interested in but your business."

She avoided looking at me or at the landscape paintings on the walls, she just seemed to fix her gaze somewhere in empty space.

"I'm glad of that," I said.

"It's for your own good," she went on. "We need one another, society and individuals. Neither society nor individual people can manage on their own."

I opened the door for her. When she was outside on the steps she turned and said:

"We've had a piece of confidential information. Anonymously. You apparently have three million crowns that you want to invest in some way."

It was minus fifteen degrees centigrade that morning. I tried to think of an answer to give her, I even opened my mouth to say something, but the only thing I managed to get out was a gigantic cloud of breath. Even today I don't know what response I should have made to her.

I could have told her that if she stayed for a while she could hear the whole story of the Madonna.

This is what Dieter Goldmann said in his letter:

His grandfather had been a butcher. He had lived in Erlangen, not far from Nuremberg. His little butcher's shop was near Hugenottenplatz, and his specialities were sausages and pies. As early as the turn of the century he began various experiments in the evenings and at nights to use new raw materials in the manufacture of his products. He wanted to transform everything that until then had been called "offal" into acceptable food, even delicacies. It was mainly skin and udders and guts and heads and gristle and tripe that he refined into paté, salami and sausage. His business expanded during the First World War, he bought scraps and offcuts from other butchers, as far afield as Bayreuth and Bamberg, and the new products were labelled "luxury quality". He also constructed a machine that could crush bone and skin to a pink pulp that was absolutely splendid for Teewurst and Bavarian Leberkäse. By the time peace came he was a rich man. He had discovered that when animals are ground down finely enough and boiled long enough, they all in the end taste the same.

Dieter Goldmann's father, Werner Goldmann, was then twenty. He had passed his school-leaving examinations, and in due course would take over the firm. His dearest wish was to be an artist. He had seen Dürer and Grünewald in the Museum of Prints and Drawings in Erlangen, and Grünewald's crucifixion scenes and La Tour's little Madonna had marked him for life. He himself painted watercolours. In the spring of 1920 he managed to persuade his father to pay for a trip to Paris. He would have two months of freedom and artistic experience before he finally buried himself in sausages and pies.

In Paris he rented a little room next to the synagogue on the rue de la Victoire. He went to museums, sat in parks and sketched, but mostly he was to be found in the bars Rotonde and Dome. There he met Fernand Léger.

One evening Léger took him to see a good friend of his who lived in an attic on the rue Lepic. There was a party in progress, a dozen artists of all nationalities eating and drinking and shouting; a few models were there too, and guests came and went with no order or coherence, many of them trying to do at least a dozen parties that same evening. The host's name was Nils von Dardel, and according to Léger he was a Swedish aristocrat who occasionally passed the time by painting. He appeared to drink as much as all the others but never got drunk; he went round with a glass in his hand smiling and telling jokes.

Dieter Goldmann's father felt somewhat alien in this company, and he sat down by the window in the little dining room; the walls were decorated with paper depicting Chinese birds and the table was covered with a Persian shawl. He looked out over the roofs of the houses, the Sacré Coeur was close by, and the haze over the Seine was illuminated from below by the street lights.

Suddenly he noticed that it had gone quiet around him. All the others had gone, and only he and Dardel were left. Dardel asked him if he wanted to see a painting, a picture that Dardel described as problematical and worrying. They spoke German, and Dardel used the word "*bedenklich*".

It was the Madonna. Dieter Goldmann's father was deeply impressed. The central figure of the triptych, the mother of God, was exactly like La Tour's Madonna that he had admired as a boy in Erlangen. She was the most beautiful person he had ever seen.

He said as much to Dardel, with tears in his eyes.

Dardel had actually intended to donate the painting to the little church of Saint-Blaise in Neufchatel, where his family came from, but he doubted whether the church would accept the gift. And he was all too aware of his own pride and dignified sensitivity, he would go mad if he was rejected.

But Dieter Goldmann's father assured him that the triptych was the most distinguished and brilliant painting he'd seen since he came to Paris.

"Yes," said Dardel, "she's really beautiful."

"I didn't believe that such beauty was possible," said Dieter Goldmann's father. "A vision of a familiar yet inaccessible paradise, as Schopenhauer put it."

"She serves in a bar called the Vigne aux Moineaux," said Dardel. "You can meet her. She's from Montesson and her name is Gertrude."

And when dawn lifted the shroud of darkness that had enveloped Paris overnight, Dieter Goldmann wrote in his letter from Karlstad, there were my father and Nils von Dardel at a table in the Vigne aux Moineaux being served a *crémant* by the Madonna, Gertrude, the girl who bore the same name as the blind girl in Gide's *Pastoral Symphony* and who would later be my mother.

"I give her to you," said Nils von Dardel.

"Thank you," said Dieter Goldmann's father. And he stayed on at the bar, it was almost true to say that he took up residence there. Nils von Dardel drank two glasses, and then left.

In two weeks everything was decided, they got engaged and she was to go with him when he returned to Erlangen. She loved him and was pleased to have a more secure life, and she'd always been interested in meat and sausages.

Before they left Paris they went up to Nils von Dardel's flat at rue Lepic 108.

"I want to buy the Madonna," said Dieter Goldmann's father.

"But she's already yours," Dardel replied.

"One is original," said Dieter Goldmann's father, "the other is a copy. I'm confused, I don't know which is which. I must have both."

Dardel gave a deep and surprisingly loud laugh, fetched a piece of paper and wrote out a receipt for five thousand francs. And so the triptych ended up in Erlangen.

At the foot of the receipt Dardel wrote: "*Gott segne Ihre Vereinigung*". The blessing was intended for all three of them, the engaged couple and the painting.

When the train from Paris to Nuremberg stopped in Verdun Dieter Goldmann's father took out a darning needle that his mother had given him and scratched his initials, W.G., at the bottom of the back of the right-hand panel.

The next year Werner Goldmann took over his father's business that was still so astoundingly successful.

But difficulties soon arose. Or more precisely: times got better. The customers started to demand genuine products. Werner Goldmann was forced to lower the prices of his delicatessen goods that were called "luxury quality". A couple of years later they no longer sold at all, they just lay in the warehouse behind

Hugenottenplatz going mouldy and rotten. There was after all a barely discernible, but nevertheless distinct, difference between genuine and false. The Goldmann family's refined palates couldn't perceive it, but it didn't escape the gustatory senses of their ordinary customers.

He couldn't afford to keep the house in Bismarckstrasse, and so the Goldmanns moved to a small flat up on Rückertweg.

It was then that the Madonna got her new frame; none of the walls was big enough for her any more, so he confined her in the false, deceptive frame that I found her in at the auction.

On the same day that Dieter Goldmann was born, his father dismantled the colossal mill that had ground bones and intestines and skins, and sold the parts as scrap iron.

That was 16th June 1931. There was enough money for the family's journey to Sweden a month later. He also owned shares amounting to ten thousand crowns in the venerable and solid Swedish firm of Kreuger & Toll.

Dieter Goldmann was and remained an only child. He was lying in a woven willow basket at the railway station in Krylbo when the Madonna was stolen. Werner Goldmann had ordered tickets to Karlskrona, and he was trying to explain to a railway clerk that he had never heard of Karlstad and certainly didn't intend to travel there. When he finally gave up and turned round to start carrying their luggage out to the platform – Dieter Goldmann's mother was sitting on a bench a little way off, feeling tired and ill – he discovered that the Madonna was missing.

The police were called, Werner Goldmann wept and shouted and cursed Swedish Railways and the whole thieving race of Swedes, but the painting was irretrievably gone. In due course he resigned himself to his fate, and in Karlstad he sold his Kreuger shares for a good profit and opened an insurance agency.

Dieter Goldmann wrote in his letter that he was moved and touched. He'd never seen the painting himself but he had seen his mother, and he realised that it must have been a work of art of almost unearthly beauty. And he enclosed a photograph of his mother.

91

At the foot of the back of the right-hand panel I found the letters W.G. scratched in; I hadn't noticed them before. And the woman on the photograph was undoubtedly the Madonna – I recognised the eyes and lips immediately. But she had aged and got fatter, her nose had grown larger and she had acquired a severe, even brutal, furrow in her forehead, just above the bridge of her nose. What had happened was that life had transformed her face into a sort of cheap fake. Up in one corner the year 1964 had been written in pencil. I burned the photograph.

I could have said all this to the woman from the tax office, the one who'd once been an art historian. But I didn't know that she'd be interested. I wasn't sure whether the Madonna had really made an impact on her, whether she'd been seriously smitten by her.

There was a lot I didn't know.

Now, long afterwards, I can say: Luckily I knew almost nothing.

For example, I didn't know what the bodyguard was doing with Paula at that time. Of course it was really not just one bodyguard, there were four on a rota basis. I don't know whether it was only one of them or all four. When she talks about it now she simply says her bodyguard. He forced her to go to bed with him. And she couldn't refuse, she didn't dare defend herself. Because she knew that it was absolutely necessary for her to have a bodyguard; she couldn't manage without that security.

The woman from the Inland Revenue was the district inspector. I didn't know that either. I stood for a long time on the steps watching her leave. She had an Opel Kadett. When I finally turned to go in again my hand had frozen to the door handle, and I had to tear it away forcibly.

"YOU SHOULD have entrusted everything to someone else," said Paula. "You can't manage the Madonna on your own, she's too big for you. I never have to worry, Uncle Erland takes care of whatever needs doing."

She continued to appear in the restaurant, she rehearsed during the day, and she was going to go on tour in the provinces in the spring and summer. I always knew what she was doing; I felt secure as far as Paula was concerned.

"You don't understand," I said, "what responsibility I have for the Madonna. Finding her is almost the same as having painted her."

I didn't want to say so to Paula, but I often thought that the Madonna was my creation through and through, not Dardel's.

The winter was unusually cold, fewer customers came than normal, I didn't have to work in the frame-shop more than two or three hours a day. Paula had sent me Debussy's *Iberia*, and I listened to it over and over again. It was played by the London Philharmonic, and it was just the sort of music I needed right then. It doesn't have any major themes nor any symmetry, nothing is regular or fixed. The sounds are merely themselves and nothing more, they don't lead anywhere, and the harmonies shift the whole time and the keys are constantly changing. It's simply a sequence of events, impossible to anticipate. All the instruments are alone, they have to be self-reliant in the midst of everything else that is indeterminate and elusive and fleeting.

Listening to *Iberia* I thought to myself: Everything is going to be fine, because anything at all can happen.

I didn't answer the letters from Dieter Goldmann and Maria, the girl who insisted that she was still living with me. But I constantly thought of what I would reply; I would have to respond some time anyway. I would be polite and understanding, but in a vague and slightly playful way; I didn't want them to imagine for a moment that their letters had upset me or that I took their claims seriously. I might perhaps be able to use the same letter for both of them. We're all like new-born babies, I thought of writing, expecting happiness and pleasure, but chance soon has us in its grip and teaches us that nothing is ours. It owns everything, all property and all relations and friends, our arms and legs and eyes, even the nose we have in the middle of our face.

The cold dispersed at the end of February, and at times I was even able to have a window open in the shop. One day as I was standing at my bench I suddenly heard somebody calling to me through the window.

"Good morning. What are you doing?"

It was her. The tax inspector.

"A family photo," I replied. "Silver frame and glass. Five generations."

"Good heavens," she said, "I didn't think that could happen. Five generations!"

"There's a photo of six generations in Magdeburg," I said. "Their name was Raublitz."

I'd read *The Guinness Book of Records* from cover to cover, of course.

"May we come in?" she asked.

"It's open," I said. "I'm open till five."

I didn't count them as they came in. There were five or six of them. She introduced them, but afterwards I couldn't recall any names or titles. One of them was the local magistrate or his deputy, a couple were policemen, I think one was called a chief investigator. They stood in the middle of the room and looked around.

"Welcome," I greeted them.

And then I told them what the genuine oil paintings cost. "The Madonna in the window is not for sale."

I don't remember what we said after that; mostly they talked among themselves and none of them took much notice of me. I sat down on the stool that I usually stood on when I moved the picture hooks up by the cornices. They had black plastic sacks that they filled with anything portable they could find, catalogues and price lists, prospectuses, notebooks and my grandfather's indecipherable drawings, and packs of cards that I used for playing patience. They emptied out all the drawers and trays and folders, they even took the latest issue of *This Week* that Paula's mother had brought that morning. It said on the cover that Paula had finally found love.

"This is a hell of a job," one of them said, and it sounded as if he was trying to comfort me. "If only people wouldn't collect so much paper around them. I tell everyone I know to burn every scrap so that there's not the slightest little truth or lie left."

One of them brought over a small piece of cardboard and showed it to me. Written on it were the numbers 583×759.

"What's this?" he asked.

"It's a picture," I said. "One of an elk bull and cow and their little calf."

"That's 442,497 if you do the multiplication," he said. "That's a lot of money."

"It's not money," I said. "It's millimetres."

"We'll see," he said. "We'll see about that."

And the oldest of them, a man in a dark suit and grey tie who looked as if he were taking part in some solemn ritual, told me that I would eventually be grateful to them. "When you get everything in order," he said. "When we've unravelled the whole tangled mess. But it'll take a while. It needs patience, like one of those little games where you have to get two balls to roll down into the eyes of a crocodile."

I had a feeling all the time that I should have shown them that they weren't upsetting or insulting me. I could have played *"O Sole Mio"* to them. But I just sat quietly on the stool.

Finally the inspector came over to me, the girl who had written a thesis on art history before she grew up. *Dreams Beneath an Arctic Sky.*

"We'll have to take the Madonna," she announced. "As security. Against all the tax debts we can presume you to have."

She had large red blotches on her cheeks, as if she was feverish, and her eyelids were quivering. She was pressing her hands to her breast so that I wouldn't see them trembling. She looked me straight in the eyes.

"I believe you," I said. "I believe in all of you."

It was true, I did believe in them. That was why I was so calm. Belief helped me.

"She's really no more than a painting," she said. "A triptych."

"I have never in my life been false or dishonest," I said.

I don't know why I said that.

She gave some kind of answer, but I couldn't hear it, because at that very moment the burglar alarm went off, the device that was intended to alert the police if anyone tried to take the Madonna. I only saw that she was smiling and her lips were forming a long sentence about nobody questioning my integrity but that they wanted to be thorough and scrupulous precisely because I was so unfathomably, not to say frighteningly, honest. And I said that I was ashamed, everything was my fault, I should have had a cash register and book-keeping and an auditor and a proper bank account – but she didn't hear what I said.

The two policemen who were taking the Madonna didn't know about the alarm, but when it went off with its air-raid warning sound one of them immediately pulled a pair of pliers out of his pocket and cut a couple of wires that I hadn't even seen. It obviously wasn't the first time they'd carried out a task of this nature. Then they bore her away.

They left, and I remained sitting on the stool – for how long I don't know. I thought I should ring the insurance company and report that the Madonna had been stolen. But perhaps stolen wasn't the right word. Deep down I had probably never believed that I would be allowed to keep her.

Finally I raised my eyes and looked at the empty shop window. I have never before seen such emptiness. It was dreadful to see the sheet of plywood that she had stood on. And the reflector lamps. I couldn't bear it so empty.

As I climbed up into the window and sat in her place, I noticed that my whole body was trembling with weariness; I sank down with my legs crossed under me, rested my head on my clasped hands and fell fast asleep almost straight away even though my eyes were still open.

I don't know why I'm writing this. Everyone has been through more or less the same sort of thing.

I certainly filled the space in a way, but of course I could never replace her. I must have looked like a waxwork figure. No customers came to see me. Or maybe customers came that I neither saw nor heard. I don't know.

When I came to it was dark, it could even have been the middle of the night. Somebody was standing outside the window looking at me. I couldn't see, but I could feel it, and that was what had woken me. I sat up and put my thumbs up to my ears and waggled my fingers and made the maddest grimaces I could produce. I wanted to demonstrate that I wasn't odd or insane, that my sitting in the window wasn't meant to be taken seriously. Then I went and opened the door.

It was the girl, the inspector. It had rained on her hair, which was hanging down over her cheeks like withered grass.

She didn't say a word, she just went straight through the shop and workshop and up the stairs to my flat. She must be going to fetch something they forgot to take, I thought.

When we got to the kitchen she took off her coat and threw it over a chair.

"I'm absolutely beside myself," she said, "I don't know what to do with myself."

She didn't need to say it, I could see it. And I felt I ought to comfort her.

"Things are only as they should be," I said. "We're hardly ever inside ourselves, we go in and out all the time."

"When the men carried the Madonna away today," she said, "that was the most upsetting action I've ever been involved in. I've just run twelve miles on the running track. But it didn't help."

"Where is she now?" I asked. "The Madonna."

"She's at the magistrate's office. That's the safest place on earth. You needn't worry."

"I never worry," I said. "But it's dreadfully empty now she's gone. She was like a mother to me."

I was obviously upset too, otherwise I'd never have said that.

"I couldn't have imagined this," she said. "That I would be taking part in such an action. It felt as if I was involved in creating something much bigger than myself."

She took a few steps towards me and started tearing at my clothes. I could feel her trembling.

"As if I were part of a work of art," she went on.

"You can never really know," I said. "It's chance that decides all the time. Not letting chance guide things is simply to leave everything to another chance."

When she pulled me over to the bed in the alcove I didn't even try to resist, I felt sorry for her, I wanted to do my best for her sake.

I'd got myself a wide bed with an interior spring mattress when that woman Maria had been living with me.

She kept repeating my name the whole time, but I never said hers; I'd forgotten what she was called, I didn't want her to have a name. It felt strange to be making love with her, as if I wasn't quite sure whether she was a normal woman or a representative of the authorities.

Actually none of this can have been as complicated or involved as it sounds here. I wish I could write the way Glenn Gould used to play.

But while I was doing my utmost to help her I suddenly remembered that it was my turn to phone Paula that evening. I raised myself up on my elbows to look at the clock. It was half past midnight.

I asked her to excuse me for a moment, I just had to hurry down and do something, I'd be back soon, it had slipped my mind because my thoughts had been elsewhere. Then I ran down to the telephone in the shop.

Paula didn't believe me when I told her that they'd taken the Madonna. "Things like that don't happen here," she said. "Not in Sweden."

When I came back upstairs the tax inspector was lying exactly as she had been, so I was able to carry on from where I'd left off.

It took a couple of hours before she was relaxed and satisfied and had recovered from her arousal. I fell asleep straight away, as wet and exhausted as if I'd just stepped out of the shower.

It was daylight when I woke up; I was freezing cold and my whole body was grey with dried sweat.

She'd gone. She hadn't slept for even a few moments beside me. Perhaps she'd wanted to be tactful and discreet, after all she'd only come because she absolutely had to.

As far as I could see she hadn't even been tired. All my art books had been taken down from the shelf and were lying in piles on the floor. She had stayed on after I fell asleep and had looked at books and read for the remaining hours of the night. On top of one of the piles was *Dreams Beneath an Arctic Sky*. When I opened it I found a dedication. It was long and very well written. If I'd still got the book I'd have transcribed it here word for word. "The greatest achievement of Surrealism," she had written, "was that it lifted the content of the consciousness out of the person and transformed it into a reality in itself, a thing. Thanks to Surrealism, the life of the soul had become visible as something external, something that concerns us only as an image, the core of personality remaining intact. Surrealism points the way to health through the realisation that the unconscious is just something we imagine. Or: something false. To put it simply, we can achieve atonement by differentiating, in the spirit of Surrealism, between the person and the thing." That was the gist of it. "Sincere appreciation and respect," she had added. "With love from the author."

I PICKED OUT another painting for the shop window. A little girl seated on a stone, crying, an old fisherman with a pipe in his mouth leaning over her, and two sailing boats lying motionless out at sea. It was signed Ström.

Ström doesn't exist. But in the studios or small factories where those kinds of paintings are produced they often write Ström down in one corner. It's a good name for an artist.

Then the journalists started ringing. They'd had a tip-off. "Of course you're innocent," they said. "Everyone is always innocent."

Five journalists in a couple of hours. They all had the same questions. And got the same answers. As I talked with the first one I noted down what I said, and then I just read out the answers when the others phoned.

Putting things in frames and under glass was the only way of creating sense and order that I knew. I'd never had a cash register or book-keeping system or an auditor, and never any proper bank account. I'd never even kept any paperwork in my pocket, I'd just had two drawers into which I'd put all the bits and pieces of paper at random. Both socially and privately I'd been slack and slovenly. It was impossible to know what amounts of money I'd failed to declare, thank goodness it was now going to be sorted out at last. Perhaps it wasn't just I myself who was guilty but the whole of my family for generations. No, I'd never been troubled by pangs of conscience. But now I felt a sense of relief and liberation. I had never understood anything, I hadn't even had the wit to suspect myself; it was a relief to be exposed at last.

I felt rather pleased with those conversations. They were short, and I was left in peace. The journalists sounded happy and satisfied too. One of them said that that was fine, the details weren't so important, it was just the main points they wanted.

The last snow fell that afternoon. I stood at the window watching it fall and thinking that it actually looked like the snow on the four-hundred or six-hundred-crown paintings. It could have been painted by Ström.

And the last customers came. But neither they nor I knew that after them there would be no more customers. They wanted an anniversary of a confirmation and a one-hundredth birthday framed.

In the evening Paula and I talked about her forthcoming tour. She was going to travel all summer. I said that I would have loved to have come with her, but who would look after the shop and the frame-making business? I had never allowed myself a holiday in my entire life. We didn't mention the Madonna.

The next day Paula's mother brought the newspapers over. She'd seen the placards down by the bus station and been curious to know who this art-dealer was. "You're not bothered about it," she said. "But for us who know you it's amazing. You're much bigger than I'd thought."

"I'm nothing," I replied. "I've never been anything."

"Just think," she went on, "I've been your neighbour all these years and never realised anything. I can't understand how you've managed to stay so modest and discreet."

"I shouldn't have put the Madonna in the window," I said. "I should never have opened that idiotic frame."

"People can't keep themselves to themselves for ever," she said. "In the end you explode from within. You have to show the whole world who you really are."

"I'm 22 by 27," I said. "I've never tried to conceal the fact. Anyone can see that."

She stared at me, her eyes wide; momentarily she very much resembled Paula.

"I didn't understand that," she said. "You and your secrets."

"If I were a painting. That's the smallest standard format. In centimetres."

"It's all so beautiful," she said. "You've never wanted to make the rest of us envious. You loathe being admired and revered. But you won't escape this time."

When she'd gone I had a look at the papers for a while. And she was right, I wouldn't escape this time. "The biggest tax fraud in the county for many decades." "Art-dealer: I am guilty." In three of the papers I had chosen to come forward and speak out.

"Yes, I'm a fraud. No one who doesn't bluff his way through the world can ever make any money."

I couldn't remember having said that.

"His voice is calm and steady," they had writen, "and he never has to pause and search for words. It's plain to hear that he is a man who knows what he wants and doesn't baulk at difficulties or resistance."

Even one of the evening papers ran a piece about me. And they had dug out the photographs of me and the Madonna.

In the afternoon I finished the aquavit I had in the house. That night Paula rang; she'd read the evening paper and wanted to console me.

"They won't break me that easily," I said. "I'll come back. You have to get used to a knock or two in business life. For God's sake."

She used words like tragedy and cruelty and grief.

"I just feel stimulated," I said. "I could take on the whole world."

And that was true.

Uncle Erland had given her a parrot, it was Australian and its name was Cassandra. Paula had already taught it two of her songs. It had a hoarse, deep and slightly threatening voice; Paula imitated it to let me hear. "I cry when you fumble around within me." I'm the only person who's heard Paula sing like a parrot.

As I sit writing this I can hear the sea in the distance all the time, and if I raise my eyes I can see the cherry tree in blossom. It has the window as a frame around it, it looks like a painting by Krouthén that has had life blown into it. In the glass by my arm I have a drink called *Für Immer Selig*. I just want to mention it. Perhaps I'm impatient to say how it all ended. Or more correctly: has ended up to now.

I framed the confirmation anniversary and the hundredth birthday, and then had nothing more to do.

Paula's mother borrowed *The Guinness Book of Records* from me. "You can have it for a couple of days," I said. But she didn't return it. After four days I went over to her and asked for it back. At first she tried to pretend that she'd forgotten she'd even borrowed it. But I stood my ground until in the end she brought it out.

"It's the best and truest book I've ever read," she said. "That's exactly how things are."

Eventually Dieter Goldmann in Karlstad and Maria, the girl who insisted that we belonged together for eternity, got an answer to their questions. "In fact," I wrote to them both, "I had already decided to send you the painting – I am, as you know, financially independent and don't need it – but the authorities intervened. It looks now as if no one owns the Madonna, and that she won't allow herself to be owned at all in the normal meaning of the word. I had already got some corrugated cardboard and thick string to wrap her up; it would have been terrible for both you and me if she had been damaged in transit. When you dream or hope something you must always be sure to imagine the opposite as well, then you'll never be disappointed, as Schopenhauer says. I hope you have applied that rule on the matter of the Madonna. And I imagine the opposite. It was good to hear from you. Yours truly," I wrote.

I thought I could at least treat them to those letters, since they had gone to so much trouble and been so full of expectation.

A policeman came with a tape recorder. It took three cassettes to tell my story; it was of course the same account as I've presented here. He said nothing. Except to say that I'd been lucky. If the authorities had read the newspapers before they moved in on me, I wouldn't have got off so lightly, they'd have emptied the house without further ado. But it wasn't easy for them to have known, journalists can always dig out details and facts that are inaccessible to the State or local authorities, since they're not bound by laws and statutes.

I missed my customers. I thought of dozens of conversational responses but had no one to make them to. And a shop and a workshop without customers is dreadfully depressing, if not tragic. People who went past in the street outside often slowed down and peered in through the window and I tried to smile at them; I often stood leaning over the paintings in the window so that they could see me properly, and I grinned and chuckled till my cheeks began to quiver with cramp, but it was no use.

Every evening Paula said: "Why don't you come here? I've got a room that's just standing waiting for you."

"Who would look after the business?" I asked. "Framing pictures is a damned sight more difficult than people think."

"You said yourself that there's no business any more. That all the customers have disappeared."

"That was just metaphorically speaking," I said. "In reality it's still there. It's been there for three generations, it can't suddenly dissolve into thin air."

"In reality it might well go up in smoke," said Paula, "but still exist metaphorically."

In fact, of course, that was what had already happened.

I wish that I could have understood Paula's world. The life she lived, the songs she sang, those abominable dresses. And her public. Then many things could have been very different. But I avoided her music and her picture in the papers, and when I heard her name on the radio or TV I switched off. I found the whole thing false and repulsive.

One newspaper wrote: "Paula's new career is one long uninterrupted orgasm."

Anyone who really wants to understand Paula's art and her music can read Per Mortensen's *Paula: The Book* (Norstedts Publishers). It's supposed to say everything.

Even if I'd still had my cash-box, it would have been empty. I used what was left of my money to buy enough packs of yoghurt and cans of pea soup to last for a few weeks.

Finally I put those two remaining pictures under my arm, the confirmation anniversary and the hundredth birthday, and walked over to the people who'd ordered them, my last customers. My car was out of petrol.

I got the same answer from both of them.

"We don't want your frames," they said. "You never know. But we'd like the photograph back."

So I carefully loosened the backs and took off the copper wire – and I had to protect the pictures because it was drizzling with rain – then I took the glass and the boxes and the empty frames back home with me. It was a bitter experience.

I also tried the bank. "Thank goodness you don't have any debts with us," was the reaction I met with. "These cases can be both painful and costly for the banks. Quite honestly we're glad that you had your business elsewhere."

"Where?" I asked. "Where do I have my business?"

"That's right," they said. "In the end your financial affairs get so complicated that you no longer know where you keep your accounts and safe-deposit boxes and bills of exchange and letters of credit."

And they thought I would do well to lie low for a while. Now that all eyes were upon me.

They seemed to have forgotten the twenty-thousand crown loan. For the moment.

I went to the Social Services that afternoon. I really did want to lie low. There were two assistants in the office, which was in a little hut behind the bus station. They sat on opposite sides of the same desk, a man and a woman. It was just a local office, a kind of branch. There were a few files in between them and an empty sandwich pack. When I mentioned my business they gave me a broad smile at first, then their cheeks started twitching, and finally they burst out laughing. They slapped their hands on the desk and jumped up and down in their seats, and I couldn't help chuckling a little, too. After a few moments they stood right up so that we could all laugh on an equal footing, so to speak. The man just managed to get out a few words to say that I shouldn't be offended, that I must understand their situation, I was the first multi-millionaire who had ever come to them, it was all too delightful a joke.

Actually I was grateful to them for receiving me like that, because the whole affair was rather embarrassing.

When we'd calmed down and I turned to go they came over to me, clapped me on the back and thanked me for coming; it was very kind of me to go to so much trouble to cheer them up, normally they only got depressing matters to deal with.

I ate the yoghurt in the mornings, and the pea soup in the evenings. The mornings were worst; I tried to sleep through them. I had stopped opening the shop. Late one evening I was sitting with my pea soup listening to Bruckner's *Requiem* when the phone rang; I thought it was Paula.

"Hi, sister," I said. "My sweetheart."

But it wasn't Paula. It was an unknown man's voice, harsh and distant, and it took a few moments before we could get a normal conversation going. He told me his name. "I don't know whether you remember me."

"I hardly remember anyone," I replied.

"I was the one you told that you'd always felt prepared for something really big to happen to you."

"And you said that the Madonna was as powerful as a hydrogen bomb," I said.

"That's right. That was me."

So that's who it was, the powerfully built little man with the goatee beard, the one who had sat for three days just staring at the Madonna.

He had seen in a newspaper what had happened.

"Have you always been prepared for this too?" he asked.

"I don't know," I said. "You can probably sense something coming all the time."

"Then you can never be really taken by surprise," he said.

"No," I said. "I don't think so."

"I have a surprise for you," he said.

"Have you?"

"But you'll have to come here. To Stockholm."

"I can't travel anywhere. I haven't got any money."

He would post me money, he even apologised for not having sent the money first and phoned afterwards. He lived at 73 Döbelnsgatan.

"I'm not used to thinking of others," he said. "I like life to be as sterile as possible. I loathe always being distracted."

But I could hear him playing Mozart: "Now at last comes the moment" was being sung by a soprano in the background.

"I bought yoghurt and pea soup with my last money," I said. "I was beginning to feel almost as if I'd been deserted."

"Things could be worse," he replied. "I like pea soup. You soon get tired of lobster and oysters and caviar."

I promised to come. He's having me on in one way or another, I thought. But it's as good as anything else.

"I don't want to know anything about your surprise," I said. "You intend to trick me. But I don't give a damn."

"Yes," he said, "but I shall trick you so beautifully and exquisitely that you will be grateful to me as long as you live."

I packed that same evening. Jacket and trousers and underpants and Schopenhauer's *On the Suffering of the World* and toothbrush and socks. And my grandfather's old dressing gown; I was going to stay with Paula.

So I had two friends in Stockholm: Paula and the man with the goatee beard. I was travelling to visit my friends in Stockholm.

That was what I said to Paula's mother. She didn't ask whether Paula was one of them. She had started playing the guitar, the same tune over and over again, "Sleep in My Arms". She bent over the guitar and pressed it to her body as if it was a little baby. Piles of *Swedish Women's Weekly* and *This Week* were scattered around her. If I could paint I would have done a big portrait of her just like that. It's the image of her I shall always remember. But of course I didn't think that then. She stopped after "Under His wing" and straightened up and said: "Yes, my dear, if only I dared. I've got thousands of friends in Stockholm. But people won't leave me in peace. And it's such trouble to travel incognito."

Then she bent forward again and continued with "Your Burning Cheek".

I WANTED TO see the Madonna one more time. I broke my journey on the way to Stockholm and went to the magistrate's office. A secretary received me.

Yes, of course, it wasn't at all out of the ordinary, I was fully within my rights, the Madonna could now be more or less regarded as public business. I was shown in to one of the magistrates, who might perhaps have been the overall boss.

She was hanging on the wall above his desk. He was wearing a dark blue suit and tie and black-rimmed glasses. After mutual greetings he said: "This is the safest place on earth. Nothing can ever be stolen from here."

"Who would steal paintings?" I said. "All art will soon be valueless."

"No, no," he replied. "Art has its ups and downs. But in the long run it's the only thing that will endure."

I asked if I could sit down for a moment. "My legs feel a bit weak," I said, "I'm not eating well and not sleeping at night."

He sat down beside me.

"It's incomprehensible," he said, "that people let themselves be treated like this. That nobody resists."

"But for God's sake," I said, "we're guilty."

"You can never know that," he said. "All investigations and court judgements are based on guesswork, nothing more."

"I know that I'm guilty, anyway," I said. "Even if no one says it to my face, I know. I'm worthless. I've never achieved anything, no one has any joy in me, the only thing I've ever striven for is to satisfy my own desires."

He brought some tea and biscuits for us. We ate and drank

without saying anything; we looked at the Madonna. After a while he said:

"I would never let it happen. I'm a collector, too, I know what I'm talking about."

I asked whether it was art he collected.

Yes, he was an art collector. Actually, that was all he was. Art was his life. Everything else was just a way of passing the time. Art was a reason for living, his job as a magistrate was at most a vocation.

"If you're really going to collect art," I said, "you need a devil of a lot of money."

Yes, that was how it had all begun. He'd inherited a fortune. And he'd realised that it had to be properly managed, that it was up to him to make something of it. It was his grandfather who'd amassed the fortune. He'd invented a windcheater made of wood pulp, during the First World War. And then one piece of clothing after another, paper clothes became an amazing success, and at one time he owned fifteen factories in Sweden and Europe. When the war was approaching its end he sold the lot. What was left was this immense fortune that his descendants had since been burdened with.

I told him about my grandfather's pianos.

"Everything depends on chance," he said. "People happened to want clothes just then, not pianos. It could equally well have been the other way round."

"If my grandfather had created a fortune like that," I said, "then things really would have been bad for me." But now I had almost nothing to break the law with.

He persuaded me to have a few more biscuits and told me not to be so miserable, my self-accusations hurt only myself, and in all likelihood I was completely innocent. In essence, and if all circumstances were taken into account, everyone was totally innocent.

"But sooner or later in every life there comes a time of examination, review and reappraisal," he said.

"There was a conductor in Vienna called Stroltzener," I said. "Once when he was conducting Bruckner's Fourth he brought in the scherzo directly after the coda in the first movement. The mistake was too much for him, he simply couldn't cope with the humiliation."

"Yes," said the magistrate. "Yes, I can understand that."

Then he told me about his collection. It was really magnificent. I would like to have seen it.

As we talked, we weren't looking at one another, we were looking at the Madonna.

"That little Christ-figure puzzles me," he said. "The crucified child. I don't understand it."

"It was just something that Dardel imagined," I said. "It was a composition, nothing more than that. He thought the child was more decorative than the adult Christ."

"Yes, but to crucify him," said the magistrate.

"That didn't bother Dardel," I replied.

Before I left he told me that everything else that had been seized and impounded was being kept in the vaults. But the Madonna was unique.

"Yes," I said. "She is."

And he was pleased that I'd looked in. "There's no one here who understands me," he said.

"Yes," I said. "I understand."

He hoped we would meet again, he thanked me for the anecdote about the conductor in Vienna, despite the fact that I'd forgotten to tell him how it all ended, and said that if I happened to be passing I must definitely call on him again.

"You never know," I said. "I'm sure I don't. Anything might happen to me, I'm not even bothering to think about it any more."

S TOCKHOLM is like a film or a television programme, all you see is fast movement and gaudy colours and pretentious faces, you're never really taking part. The underground suits me, you don't need to see anything there.

From the station I went straight to Paula's apartment. It was half past midnight: I'd taken the last train so that she would get home before I arrived.

She had bought me a crab, even though they weren't in season, and a bottle of wine that was of much higher quality than I could appreciate. She remembered how I sometimes used to buy a crab just for myself and hide up in the attic while I ate it.

Everything in her apartment was white, the furniture and the grand piano and the curtains and the record player and the mats and the lampshades and the walls. The only picture she had was a white cartoon with a gold frame round it. I suppose she'd chosen all that white as a contrast to everything else in her life. I almost felt angry when I saw it.

She had washed off all her make-up and looked more or less as I remembered her. After I'd started eating she sat down at the piano and played. It was Mahler; I knew every note. Then she began to sing. "*Ich bin der Welt abhanden gekommen.*" I am lost to the world. I'd forgotten the translation I'd done. But now I could hear that it was meant for her voice, and not just for her voice but for the whole of her little being. A lump came to my throat that almost prevented me getting the crab down.

Afterwards we sat in absolute silence. I didn't know whether there was anything I should have said.

Luckily the parrot started singing. If singing is the right word.

She was imitating Paula. She too, the parrot, was lost to the world. She had been corrupted. It was the most objectionable faking I'd come across in my entire life. Though there was no doubt that the parrot's song came from the heart; she was expressing something both for herself and for Paula. It would have been terribly cruel to laugh at her. Paula came and sat next to me and we chatted about all sorts of things while I ate the crab and drank the wine.

"How long can you stay?" she asked.

"A couple of days," I replied.

That was what I imagined, anyway.

The bodyguard was sitting in his room; he came out after a while and greeted me. Before we went to bed, he looked through the contents of my suitcase and ran his hands carefully over the outside of my clothes.

"I don't like doing this," he said. "But there are no limits to what people think up to get to Paula. It could be anything. Just to touch her or to kill her or to force her to look in their direction, they don't care."

"She's actually called Ingela," I said.

I suppose I said that to prove that I really knew her. But he just laughed, drily, like a cough.

"You don't say," he responded.

The next day Paula ordered a car for me. Paula Music Ltd had an account with Frey's Car Hire. And I drove to 73 Döbelnsgatan, to see the man with the goatee beard.

It was one of the longest journeys in my life, it took twelve minutes and my thoughts were completely clear and lucid. I was aware of every single person and every individual house, and could have described the people and the façades and the shop windows in minute detail afterwards. I was entirely in the dark about what was going to happen. Goatee probably just intended to use me as his clown or as the butt of his jokes, or perhaps he'd even forgotten that I was coming. I felt free in a strangely exhilarated way. After having lost the Madonna, I had nothing to lose.

But he was waiting for me. He took my coat and put a glass of port in my hand. He said something about wallowing in experiences of beauty and emotions, but I didn't hear it – what I saw on his walls was so overwhelming that all my senses except sight were switched off or numbed. From now on I shall definitely stick to this name, and with a capital letter: Goatee. What I did with the port wine I don't know.

There were two Cézannes hanging in the hall, a view over Mont Sainte-Victoire and a wonderful portrait of his wife; she was gazing in a slightly sad and anxious manner at two landscapes by Hodler on the opposite wall. The inside of the main door was covered with a wood-carving by Barlach, a male figure in a cloak who seemed to be taking short swift steps into the apartment. By the hat-rack there was a mirror, or rather it looked like a mirror, but when you got in front of it you discovered that it was a glass-covered painting by Dalí, a green form against a blue sky, the body held up with scaffolding and drawers sticking out of the legs. If Goatee hadn't put his arm round my shoulder and steered me in a firm but friendly way into the living-room I would have stayed in the hall for the rest of the day.

Between the two windows facing the street there was a huge Matisse, an open window looking on to a flower garden and a sea and a golden, almost luminous sky. It was the most beautiful Matisse I'd ever seen.

"He painted it in '98 on Belle-Ile in Brittany," said Goatee. "As you see, he'd already begun to take his leave of the Impressionists. He had just inherited a hundred thousand francs from an old aunt in Le Cateau."

There were also five Picassos and three Braques hanging in that room. I said nothing, nothing in all that time; I couldn't. Except that when I saw that enormous Matisse, I said "23×72."

That was pure reflex.

I think he changed the port glass in my hand for a glass of brandy – at least that was that I was clutching in my fingers when I finally sat down in an armchair and became conscious again of who and where I was.

But first he led me through four more rooms, one for van Gogh, one for Kandinsky and two rooms where the walls were shared by Degas, Gris, Picasso, Miró and Utrillo. He had something to say about every painting: where it was painted and when; the artist's relationship to alcohol at that period; or whom, singular or plural, he was making love to at the time.

He let me sink into an armchair, with a Klee hanging in front of me, a landscape with pink and blue birds. He sat down beside me, and above his chair hung a winged pendulum clock by Chagall. I tried to take a sip of my brandy but I couldn't swallow, I had to let it evaporate in my mouth.

"You haven't asked about the surprise," he said. "The one I promised you when I rang."

I could only shake my head. Which meant: You needn't go to any trouble, I can't be any more surprised than I am already.

"You may be wondering who I am," he said. "Despite all this I'm completely unknown to the general public."

I nodded. But in fact I hadn't given a thought to who he might actually be. The paintings spoke for him.

"I love art," he said. "I'm a collector. And life has been generous to me. It has given me the resources necessary to be able to acquire everything I've wanted."

I nodded again, as if to indicate that life had treated me in more or less the same way.

He didn't need to say any more. I thought I knew everything about him.

"Sensibility is the genius in each of us," he went on. "It fills us with desire and pride and helps us to see that anything which isn't slightly deformed is soulless. Sensibility makes us creative. And the more we create, the more fruitful we become."

When I nodded now, it meant that I'd recognised what he said. It was Baudelaire.

"But the world is full of people who can't think for themselves," he said. "They can only think *en masse*, as in Belgium."

Noticing then that our brandy glasses were empty, he helped me up out of the armchair and took me over to a drinks cabinet in the Kandinsky room. There he taught me how to mix the drink called *Für Immer Selig* that was invented by Emil Nolde. It was the only work of a German Expressionist that he showed me. Two parts brown ale, one part gin, one part sweet vermouth, one part angostura, a pinch of salt and a few drops of Tabasco. And then I could start talking again.

"The greatest surprise in my life," I said, "was when the authorities took the Madonna. I realised later that they had to do it, that they were right to do it. I hadn't understood what a wretch I was."

"The good thing about this drink," said Goatee, "is its lack of definition. I contains all the sourness and sweetness and saltiness and bitterness imaginable. You can let your mouth choose which taste it wants."

But I had nothing to say about *Für Immer Selig*. It's not an ingratiating drink, it takes time to get used to it.

"People just imagine they're surprised," I said. "Surprise doesn't exist in itself."

"If someone gets more than he'd hoped for, then he'll be surprised despite himself," he said. "There is no more exquisite pleasure than producing that kind of surprise."

While we were sitting talking in our armchairs he had a sketch pad on his knees, and he was still holding it. Now and then he would put his glass down and make some quick movements with his pen on the paper.

"Imagination," he said. "And ideas. And images. That's all we have. Image worshippers, that's what we are."

It was a pity that Paula hadn't come with me, I thought. She would have taken pleasure in this conversation too, and in all the art and the agreeable atmosphere surrounding Goatee.

"Beyond our ideas there is nothing," I said. "At the centre of all our ideas there is a solid nucleus. That nucleus is the world."

"Yes," he said. "That's exactly how it is."

"It wasn't I who said that," I explained. "It was Schopenhauer."

"Of course," he said. "Schopenhauer."

"The world isn't much," I said. "Not even a gas or a mist. It's more like an etching on clear glass."

We had finished our drinks. He went for a quick walk through the rooms with his sketch pad still in his hand and switched on countless numbers of reflector lamps that illuminated the paintings. It had begun to get dark. I went with him, but I didn't dare look at all the works of art; the conversation had made me feel comfortably calm and I didn't want to be upset or disturbed again.

He stopped by the little group of chairs beneath Klee and Chagall. He tore off three sheets from his sketch pad and handed them to me. They weren't signed.

They were of me. My startled head with the innocent tonsure of hair above my ears. I looked at them long and hard, one at a time.

"A Modigliani," I said. "About 1910.

"And a Picasso. Fairly late. 1930s.

"And this is a Toulouse-Lautrec. Done in the nursing home in Neuilly."

If I'd been sober and if he hadn't made me so confused, those drawings would never have existed for me. They quite simply could not exist. I raised my head and looked at Goatee.

"Mephistopheles," I said. I hadn't thought of it before, but he actually looked like Mephistopheles in Böcklin's painting.

Then he took me by the hand and led me to a little room, more of an alcove, behind van Gogh's room. He drew back a curtain and there hung the Madonna.

It really was she.

I wasn't surprised; I just registered the fact that she was hanging there. And I began to cry, despite doing all I could to control myself.

"Well, what do you say?" Goatee asked.

I said nothing; I tried to dry my eyes with my wrists. I had taken it for granted that I would never see her again.

"Look carefully," he said. "She really deserves to be inspected under a magnifying-glass. It's no accident that she's the only

Swedish painting in my exclusive little collection."

That was as it should be. No other work by a Swedish artist could have stood up to being hung with Klee and Chagall and Picasso and van Gogh.

"You don't need to tell me that," I said. "I was the one who found her."

When I'd finished sniffing, I took my magnifying-glass out of my jacket pocket and went up to her and began inspecting her milli-metre by millimetre as I'd done thousands of times before, and I could recognise every single brush stroke and every grain of paint. Seeing her again was a thousand times sweeter than it had been to see Paula.

"And yet I know that she's hanging in the magistrate's office," I said.

I was thinking to myself that he must tell me how he managed to steal her.

"Yes, indeed," he said. "She's hanging there too."

A little part of me had known all along what these masterpieces on his walls actually were. But my eyes and my intellect and my imagination refused to accept it. They were not just paintings by the greatest artists. They were the greatest painters' greatest works.

"I'm very proud of the Madonna," he said. "I've never been better. No one would believe that I'll soon be sixty-five."

"Matisse was seventy-eight when he painted *The English Girl*," I said. "Picabia was nearly eighty when he did *I Never Want to Paint Again*."

"Picabia," he said. "It's funny that you should mention him. I haven't got a Picabia."

"You ought to have," I replied.

"There isn't time for everything," he said. "And I can perhaps be content with what I've achieved."

"Yes," I said. "I would be happy if I'd done a thousandth part of it." I was still looking at the Madonna through the magnifying-glass, and it wasn't all that easy to talk to him at the same time.

"No other Swedish artist is represented in so many of the big museums as I am," he said. "In Europe and the U.S.A. And Japan. The really major paintings."

"Well, well," I said. What else could I say?

"If you look an inch below the point of the dagger," he said, "you'll see a crimson spot. A tenth of a millimetre in diameter."

"Yes," I said, "I can see it. I never saw that little pinprick when she was with me."

"That's my signature," he said. "It's the only thing that distinguishes it from the Madonna in the magistrate's office."

"It doesn't matter," I said. "That microscopic little dot."

"Even when we have achieved the utmost perfection we are still vain," he said. "We never learn to wear our genius with humility."

And he told me a story:

He was in London, standing with a group of people in one of the most famous museums; they were admiring an Impressionist cityscape, mist and street lights and the Seine. Finally he could contain himself no longer, and said:

"I painted that."

But nobody seemed to hear him. So he raised his voice. And some of them looked at him and smiled. In the end he shouted as loud as he could: "I was the one who painted that!" And he leaned forward and tried to indicate the tiny crimson dot. But warders came and grabbed him by the hands and feet and carried him off, all the way down the stairs and through a back door, and put him out among the dustbins. "The martyrdom of genius," he said.

"People are disgusted by forgeries," I said. "Like rats or corpses."

I probably shouldn't have said that. He suddenly shook his fist at me and stuck out his chin so that his beard pointed at my breast like a dagger.

"Forgeries!" he yelled. "Have you seen a single forgery on my walls?"

"No," I said. "Absolutely not."

He began to lecture me then at length; his voice was shrill, almost threatening.

"Of all the work that an artist produces, only half at most is genuine. Not even Picasso was able to paint a genuine Picasso every time. But I have never had a failure, a Klee by me is a genuine Klee, there isn't the slightest little weakness or flaw in my Dalís and Matisses and Chagalls. It's a question of the transubstantiation of paint: the paint must be transformed and turned into something higher and more wonderful than itself."

I had to agree. It was true.

"Authenticity is a quality of the work of art, it has nothing to do with who created it," he went on. "No artist has to apply himself so rigorously to the question of authenticity as one who creates the paintings of others. He has to be up to the standard he's painting at. I have to be not just Léger and Braque and La Fresnaye, I have to be the whole of the art of painting. It's a matter of empathy. Empathy and technique. Do you understand?"

"I'm really only a picture-frame maker," I replied.

"You have to give authenticity a new and deeper meaning," he roared. "Unmask conventional bourgeois authenticity and at the same time raise and refine so-called falsehood to reveal a hitherto unknown and singular freedom, a state of indifference and relativity. I simply create freedom. Freedom from certainties and markets and the authorities. What are called forgeries are the only true expression of our age. Can you comprehend what I'm saying?"

I'm not sure that I understood him. But he was so touching and grandiloquent in his excitement that I really wanted to do my best, so I nodded and smiled at him as emphatically as I could. But it was no use.

"Don't you see that all the difficulties and horrors in our lives are based on our inability to come to terms with the problem of falsehood and authenticity?" he shrieked, his voice sliding up into a falsetto. "Only when we have levelled out or eradicated all the differences between genuine and false, only when we have created an existence for ourselves of definitive uncertainty and doubt, only then will we be able to live happily. Happily ever after."

Then he turned on the Madonna. He put her down on the floor

and broke off the frame, he kicked the corners so that the glue gave way and the pins snapped, and he trampled on the mouldings till the gilding flaked off and the wood split. "If anyone should have appreciated me and understood me it was you," he cried. "When I saw what the authorities had done to you, I thought to myself: he is a gift to me, I shall make him happy, I shall give him back all that he has lost. He will be able to say to the authorities: 'It doesn't matter what you take from me, you can go off with everything I have and everything I own, I will always be able to find a replacement.' But all you have to give me is your stupid provincial grin and a few miserable tears. You really are as simple as you say you are."

Even today I still don't know what he had really expected of me.

He folded up the three parts of the Madonna, banged them together so roughly that I could hear the little hinges groaning, and handed her to me – no, he threw her into my arms.

"Take her and get out of here," he said. He pushed me through the Kandinsky room and the van Gogh room to the outer door. "You might even have loved me," he said.

All I could think of to say was: "But it's true that I'm guilty, I've only myself to blame, I really am a cheat."

How I got home to Paula's I don't remember. I presumably managed to get hold of a taxi down on Döbelnsgatan or on Sveavägen.

Paula wasn't at home, but she'd given me a key. "You must keep it," she said. "I won't ever want it back."

I placed the Madonna on the little wall-mounted writing shelf in my room and opened her out and directed the desk lamp and reading lamp at her. I can't remember what I thought. Perhaps I thought that some kind of higher power, a power other than chance, had intervened to bring me back to a life of beauty. I could make a new frame when I got her home, exactly like the one Goatee had made, which was the same as my original one, the genuine one, in every detail. I was obviously destined to be happy. I had really got the Madonna back again.

I F I SCREWED up my eyes and concentrated on the area below the tip of the dagger I thought I could almost see the crimson dot. But I wasn't sure. And it wasn't significant.

When Paula came in after rehearsals she'd bought a local paper from back home. There was a little article about me on the front page. My case would soon be concluded. I would probably be found completely innocent. Dardel's famous painting of the *Madonna with the Dagger* would be restored to me. Along with everything else. For its part the paper deeply regretted any impression it might have given in earlier articles that I was guilty of serious financial crimes. Mistakes are inevitable in news reporting. No one could be more sincerely pleased at my exoneration than this newspaper.

"Isn't it wonderful?" said Paula.

"It's a trap," I said. "They've discovered that I've disappeared. Now they're trying to trick me into returning."

Paula had never seen the Madonna. She had seen photographs, but never met her in reality. We sat before her now right up to the moment when Paula had to go off to her performance. We ate the pizzas the bodyguard had brought for us. I can't remember our saying anything – perhaps we were embarrassed about the words we would have had to use. I told her about Goatee as straightforwardly as I could. "He's not just an individual painter," I said, "he's the whole of modern art." Paula asked no questions, she didn't even seem surprised. The world she lived in was like that: nothing existed in itself, everything represented something else. I had never told her how deeply I hated that world.

One should feel a certain despair at a work of art that is both authentic and fake. But I just felt peaceful and gently elated; for me she was as genuine as a painting or a person or a performance ever can be, and since she was a forgery nobody would want to bother taking her away from me. I think that Paula's thoughts and feelings went along roughly the same lines. And I had really done nothing to deserve her, I realised that; she was actually too good for me.

Night had fallen by the time Paula came home, and I was still sitting on the floor with my legs tucked under me, maybe having dozed off occasionally for a few minutes at a time. She put a cushion on the floor and came and sat beside me.

When she said: "I think of her sometimes, I wonder how she is," I knew immediately whom she was talking about. She had always found it difficult to say the words "Mother" or "Mum".

"You needn't worry," I replied. "She's fine. She's started playing the guitar. 'Sleep in My Arms'."

"She's tone deaf," said Paula. "It must be dreadful."

"She has to practise," I said. "But she's getting better and better."

We chatted about everything back home, people and events and the countryside and the music shop and the framing business, and suddenly our houses on the road between the church and the bus station seemed as remote to me as they had for many years to Paula. I tried to tell her how life had changed over the last few years for those of us who had stayed there, but actually I didn't know whether anything had changed at all. We were looking at the Madonna the whole time; I liked seeing her without a frame, she seemed simpler and more like the rest of us.

"Even as a forgery she's infinitely better than any other Swedish painting," I said. "If I'd dared, I'd have asked Goatee to do one for you, too."

"I don't want to own anything," said Paula.

I knew that. And in fact I felt the same; it wasn't in order to own the Madonna that I wanted to have her.

Stockholm is surprisingly quiet for a couple of hours in the early hours of the morning. All we could hear was a cassette player in the bodyguard's room. He'd recorded one of Paula's concerts himself, "I Suck the Whole World". I don't remember everything we talked about. We were sensitive, receptive and eloquent.

Paula told me she had met Somebody. No one but me was to know that there was a Somebody.

It was very simple. She herself used the word trivial. It could have been a story in a women's magazine. Uncle Erland hadn't been happy about her eyes. Or rather, he'd wanted her eyes to be even bigger, to look even more surprised and lost. So he took her to a plastic surgeon. This was some months before her return to public life. The surgeon ran a private clinic in a big manor house somewhere in central Sweden. She put it exactly like that: somewhere in central Sweden. That was all she knew. No one was allowed to know anything more. Not the newspapers nor the authorities nor competitors.

Patients were driven there in the clinic's own car, a nurse put a blindfold over their eyes, and the drive included two hours on winding gravel roads. No other private business requires such discretion as plastic surgery. Indeed, discretion, not to say a kind of freemasonry, is a part of the treatment. He had explained it to her: the black blindfold, the darkness, the restful journey and the eventual return, opening her eyes, and the new or improved face that she would finally see in the mirror; everything would be reminiscent of the dual concepts of death and resurrection, extinction and rebirth.

He had put her to sleep and made those small cuts in the corners of her eyes. She had to remain lying down with her face bandaged for a few days; they let her listen to Rimsky-Korsakov's *Russian Easter* – that was included in the treatment.

He was amazed himself when he saw what he'd created with his innocent little operation; in fact not only amazed, but seriously in love. He bent over her, holding in his hand the bandage that he'd just removed, and she lay quite still, her cheeks trembling slightly. She looked even more wide-eyed and overtly perplexed and defenceless than she had before.

This, then, was what she herself told me as we sat on the floor in front of the Madonna, sitting the way you do in front of an open fire.

She felt that she'd had no choice. Having so unreservedly offered up her face to him she had no right to withhold herself.

"I thought your eyes had got bigger of their own accord," I said.

"Maybe," she said. "I don't know. I'm not even sure that he really made those cuts. But the experience itself makes you open your eyes much wider than before, you can't help it."

I've let Paula read everything I've written so far. She laughed quite a few times. But then she said: "I sometimes wish you had more of a sense of humour."

"I still wouldn't dare use it," I replied. "I think it's the last defence we have. We should save it for a matter of life or death."

The surgeon was twenty years older than Paula, and married with four children. They used to meet at his consulting rooms on Strandvägen in Stockholm. The bodyguard had to wait outside in the car.

She wanted me to know about it. In case she didn't always come home when she should. In case I wondered about the things the newspapers wrote.

"I never read what the newspapers write about you," I said. "I'm really pleased for your sake. You need someone to take care of you."

And I remember reaching out and patting her on the back.

"All those men in my life," she said, "millionaires and lawyers and politicians and tennis players: I don't know a single one of them. They're just Uncle Erland's inventions. I've slept with a couple of sound technicians, that's all."

I didn't know what to say. What had happened between her and the plastic surgeon was fine and beautiful. I understood her. An almost irresistible temptation was concealed deep within the craft – no, the art – of a plastic surgeon.

"There's nothing wrong with sound technicians either," I said.

125

Those early morning hours on the floor in front of the Madonna had an air of unreality about them; we were entirely alone in the world. I wish I knew how to put such vague and elusive feelings into words.

She said nothing about what the bodyguard used to do to her.

"A woman called Jeanne Orvan has had nineteen face-lifts," I said. "She lives in Nevers. She's had her nose rebuilt four times, she's had eight new sets of eyebrows, tucks in her eyelids five times and double chins removed four times. Over two thousand incisions and stitchings." I think Paula was pleased that I'd actually read *The Guinness Book of Records* that she'd sent me.

When the morning papers thumped down on the hall floor Paula got up and said goodnight. She usually slept with the newspapers over her face, she said. But I stayed sitting where I was. If I'd been able to defend myself against the ironically arbitrary chance that steers the course of my life, I'd still be sitting there now.

I WASN'T COMPLETELY immobile, of course. But I stayed in the room: I couldn't bring myself to leave her alone. I was grateful to Goatee, not just for having restored her to me, so to speak, but also for his sensitivity in the way he did it. By kicking the frame to pieces and throwing her at me so carelessly or angrily he had diminished and devalued his action so that I didn't need to feel any debt of gratitude. There was no umbilical cord still connecting her to him. My life was no longer banal, it had become authentic again.

Paula brought food in, and sometimes I ate in the kitchen with her and the bodyguard. Pizzas. Kebabs. Hamburgers with prawn salad. Falafel. I got used to most of it. When I left the door open I could listen to music on Paula's stereo. She had the complete works of Brahms. He had seemed slightly alien to me before, but now I was beginning to appreciate him. I played the Allegro of the Third Symphony over and over again; that's how unpredictable everything in life can be.

One day during that period something happened that doesn't really belong here, but since I'm writing this anyway I'll include it in passing.

Paula's father was found.

I've probably mentioned earlier that a weekly magazine had offered a reward of twenty thousand crowns to anyone who found him. It must have been Crackshot who thought the whole thing up: he had a supreme sense of what would tug at heartstrings or bring lumps to throats.

It was actually Paula's father who found himself. He happened to come across an issue of the magazine in a dustbin in a boarding house in Helsingborg. He'd realised immediately: That must be me.

Of course he'd known about Paula. And he must have suspected who she was and so who he must be himself. But it had lacked significance for him. He's been busy enough on his own account. He'd done nothing but travel around in Scandinavia and northern Europe for all those years, he'd played in pubs and fringe theatres and at markets, he'd never had any fixed abode or any work permit, nor even any definite identity. Solo artist   that was what he called himself. Now he was coming to Stockholm to pick up this particular fee too. There wasn't an ounce of sentimentality in him. He is the only completely happy person to appear in this account. So far.

Uncle Erland had phoned to warn Paula.

There was a reporter and a photographer. And Paula's father.

She came in to me and asked: "How the devil shall I know whether it's really him?"

I followed her out to the living-room. He was sitting in one of the white armchairs, and wore a dirty, stained black suit, yellowing shirt and grey tie. He was looking at *Paula: The Book*, without seeming to be particularly interested in it.

Crackshot had had a magnificent biography of Paula published.

The long red hair had gone and the face had thinned and he looked smaller than before; he hadn't been consumed by his frenetic life, but he had dried up somewhat.

"Yes," I said. "That's him."

He raised his head and stared at me, squinting at me the way he always used to do and pointing with his long, outspread fingers, and asked: "Who is this character meant to be?"

"We were neighbours," I replied. "You taught me to play the mandolin. *'O Sole Mio'*."

He closed his eyes for a moment; he appeared to be searching his memory.

"You had an uncontrollable little finger," he said. "It stuck upwards all the time."

"It still does," I replied. "But I practise as often as I can."

"Hot water is best," he said. "And string round the other fingers."

128

"Yes," I said. "But I don't play seriously. Only when everything else is impossible."

Then the reporter and photographer took over. Paula and her father posed by the grand piano, he playing and she singing – and in the armchair, she sitting on his knee and pressing her cheek against his – and in the kitchen, she beating something in a bowl and he standing at the cooker with a frying pan and spatula. I enjoyed being a spectator; they were two professionals acting with a sureness and precision that could only be admired. He played not a single note on the piano and she opened her mouth without uttering so much as a whisper, and the bowl she was beating in was empty and there was nothing in the cold frying pan, and when she appeared to press her cheek to his she touched him flesh to flesh for less than a second. It was a joy to watch them.

I wondered what Paula's mother would do when she saw the article. She would cry. That was the only thing I could be certain of. She would rush off with the magazine in her hand to show to every single person she caught sight of. And she would cut out the picture of the bowl and frying pan and hang it up with a drawing pin in the kitchen.

When the whole of this moving reunion was over – Paula had even provided a tearful close-up – and they were standing out in the hall, ready to go, Paula's father asked:

"One thing that's been bothering me: were you really called Paula?"

"No," she answered. "My real name is Ingela."

"Of course," he said. "I'd forgotten. That's what it was. Ingela."

Paula was worried about me. She thought I should be doing something; I think at times she imagined I was ill. She didn't understand that I was quite simply as happy as I possibly could be at that time.

One afternoon she brought in a score, Bach's *In Praise of Truth*. It had been discovered a few months earlier, after several years of searching high and low in all the archives and likely hiding places in what was now the new Germany. The newspapers had written a lot about this cantata. It was in a trunk that had belonged to the secret police, that should really have contained a list of informers and betrayers in Leipzig, primarily the Altstadt.

"If only I had a translation," said Paula. "Then I could sing it."

Lob der Wahrheit.
Was mir behagt, ist nur die Wahrheit.
Wer bei der Wahrheit bleibt
Für immer selig ruhet
In Gottes Hand.

I tried translating it that same evening. But Paula wasn't satisfied, it wasn't singable. I couldn't manage the diphthongs.

In praise of truth.
All I desire is truth.
He who abides by the truth
Will rest at peace for ever
In the hands of the Lord.

"You ought to go for a walk," Paula said. "Stockholm is wonderful at this time of year."

"You never go for walks," I replied. "You use Frey's Hire Cars."

"I can't," she said. "But when all this is over, I'm going to spend every day from morning till night walking up and down the streets."

"What do you mean? When it's all over?"

"I don't know," she replied. "It's just something I imagine to myself."

"Like when they blew up the cement factory," I said.

Between our houses and the lake there'd been a factory that manufactured blue porous concrete, and they blew it up. The concrete was found to cause cancer. She was four, and sat on my shoulders to watch it. It was beautiful.

130

"Yes," she said. "Something like that."

On the last evening I spent at Paula's apartment she suddenly started talking about herself.

I'll say in a moment why that particular evening was the last.

This is roughly what she said:

"My life is entirely vicarious. I'm like one of those wooden birds that the hunters used to put on the lake when they were shooting duck. They looked absolutely real."

I'd forgotten the decoy ducks. It was my grandfather who'd carved and painted them and sold them round local farms. That was when he'd finally put his pianos behind him.

"I myself don't exist," she went on. "I sometimes have to look in the newspapers to find out what I've been doing and what I'm like. Or rather: not me but the person bearing my name. Though it actually isn't my name."

"Yes," I said. "It must be pretty hard for you."

"And if I say I'd rather be like this or like that, I'm immediately helped by the producer or the designer and Uncle Erland and the make-up girl to take on exactly that look. But it doesn't help. I don't even have a surname. I'm imprisoned in a bloody great mass of alien skins. If only I knew how they think they'll eventually get rid of me."

"But when you're alone with him?" I said. "The plastic surgeon."

"Yes," she said. "Then I'm myself. For a few seconds each time."

I tried talking to her as if I was taking in what she said. But I didn't really understand anything, I was just pretending. I didn't want to understand Paula's life, it repelled me. This compressed, explosive falsehood. Everyone else knew it much better. That's why I'm not writing about it.

In the end she thought of a way of helping me. She couldn't bear to see me living in my room like a prisoner.

"Perhaps if you could take her with you," she suggested.

"It's no good," I replied. "It would be all too easy to snatch her out of my hands. They don't even need to know that she's a real Dardel, they'll take her anyway. People take everything here."

But she spoke to the bodyguard about it. And he came back that very same evening with it all arranged.

"That's what we're here for," he said. "We have experience of absolutely everything. There's no security problem that we can't solve."

It was a case. It was as if tailor-made for the folded Madonna. It looked like an ordinary black leather briefcase, but there was a metal frame beneath the leather. It needed two different keys to lock it. Attached to the handle was a metal chain and a handcuff.

"There's a goldsmith on Hamngatan," he said. "He has eight million crowns' worth of diamonds in his false teeth. You can guess who made those for him."

"This metal chain," I said, "they'll simply snip it off."

"I'd like to see the metal cutters that can do that," he said. "There isn't a tool in the world that can cut into that alloy. Not a saw nor cutters nor even an oxy-acetylene torch."

"Now you can carry her with you wherever you like," said Paula. "You'll have complete freedom of movement."

"Yes," I said, "that's fantastic. Though I can't afford it. It must cost a fortune."

"It won't cost you a thing," she said. "Paula Music Ltd is paying."

"The cost," said the bodyguard, "is something you should never think about. Not when it's a question of security. You simply can't put a price on security."

PAULA WENT off to her rehearsals in the morning, and I folded the Madonna and put her in the case and locked both the locks. I fastened the handcuff on my wrist and locked it, and put the keys on the bedside table. It occurs to me now that they might still be lying there.

I drove to the Museum of Modern Art in one of Frey's Hire Cars. When I leaned the case against my knees I could rest my chin on it. The church on Skeppsholmen was shimmering like a golden apple against the light, and I suddenly realised that I was sitting there smiling with gratitude towards Paula and the bodyguard.

At first they didn't want to let me in to the museum. I would have to leave the case, they said. But when I showed them that it was impossible, that the case couldn't be opened and that it and I were inseparably united, they let me in.

I sat the whole morning in front of Dalí's *Enigma of William Tell*.

The tax inspector with the tousled blond hair, the writer of *Dreams Beneath an Arctic Sky*, should have been there too. I would have liked to talk to her about Dalí's paranoiac-critical method, that mysterious power that led him to Surrealism. All thought stems from morbid scepticism, I would have said to her. If we believed in the world, we wouldn't need to think. But once we've begun to think, we discover that our suspicions were well-founded, that we were right even before we started thinking. And that our thoughts can produce absolutely anything. Dalí was a thinker of the same type as Schopenhauer. Man needs nothing more than a palace and a park full of wild animals and a private airfield. And I would have mentioned that sometimes now I was reminded of her when I saw paintings of naked human flesh.

Paula had given me some pocket money. I had lunch in the café of the museum, cheese and ham pie. It was difficult, I had to pick up the food and pay and carry the tray and eat with just my left hand because my right hand was chained to the case. I knocked over a glass of beer at the cash desk. My left hand has always been clumsy. I've got more used to it now.

Throughout the whole day no one asked me what I had in my case. The chain around my wrist and the unusual shape of the case indicated that I was carrying something very secret, and nobody dared even bump into it.

A woman with long red hair and tinted glasses with black rims came and sat at my table. She had a large multi-coloured shawl over her shoulders and was eating the same kind of pie as I was. She was drinking red wine. She stared at the case but didn't mention it. Though actually it looked as if she was addressing the case when she said: "I eat here every day, the same pie and the same wine. You feel so safe when you know everything."

"Yes," I said, "that's just the way I like things too."

"And yet anything can still happen," she said, nodding towards the case. "You can see that all the time."

"I'm a firm believer in chance," I said.

Then she went on to tell me a secret.

She was a film historian. It was an American producer who had revealed it to her. Old films were being transferred to computer. And the computers separated out the individual, long since dead, actors, their faces, movements and voices, their complete personalities. The programme could be used to let actors who were dead and buried decades ago take part in new films; they could even be made to appear on TV interview programmes. The other participants had to learn to play to empty space, and then the computers filled the space with the dead actors so that everything looked like solid reality in the finished film. Right at this moment Drew Barrymore was featuring in a love film with Humphrey Bogart. *Eternally Yours.*

When she'd finished telling me all that, she looked at me expectantly for some time. But I didn't tell her any secrets.

I wandered around the galleries of the Modern Art Museum all afternoon. I sat down for a rest now and then; the case was heavy to carry and I've always liked to have plenty of time in galleries and museums.

Matisse has always perplexed me. I've never managed to get beneath his surface. Perhaps there's nothing more than surface to his paintings. But I still have to try, and I sat for a long time in front of his *Apollo*. But as usual I lost my concentration after about an hour and my gaze began to wander.

It was then that I noticed two young men standing off to one side behind me. And I remembered that they'd been there before while I was sitting looking at *The Enigma of William Tell*. I couldn't help smiling: Paula and the security company had obviously left nothing to chance.

At six o'clock I went along to the café again and got a cup of tea and a sandwich. I noticed that the two bodyguards followed me and sat down at the table just behind me. I didn't turn round and look at them; I realised that they didn't want their identities revealed.

I sat and looked at Edvard Munch for the last few hours. At a quarter to nine I collected my coat and went out. I was rather tired, as I usually am from seeing so many pictures in one short period. I stopped outside the museum and waited for the bodyguards; it could hardly do any harm now if I let them know that I realised who they were. I called to them as they came out.

"Over here," I shouted. "I've been waiting for you." They seemed a little hesitant, but came over to me anyway.

"I'm going to walk," I said. "The evening air. I like it."

"O.K.," they said.

"And the security firm probably wants you to follow me all the way," I said.

"Yes," they replied.

"I thought of going along Strandvägen," I said. "And then taking Styrmansgatan up to Karlaplan."

"We know a better way," they said. "We can show you."

And so we went together over Skeppsholm Bridge and along

Nybro Quay; the water in Nybroviken was as black as ink and there was a strong cold wind blowing from the direction of Djurgården. We turned off at Sibyllegatan towards Östermalmstorg. It had been a good day. I'd treated myself every year to a couple of trips to Stockholm like this, with wonderful days in museums and galleries.

"Östermalm is full of short cuts," they said. "Like tunnels in an ant hill."

"I only know the main streets," I said. "It's my memory. It's the same when it comes to art and books and music. I can never remember the small and insignificant things."

I would have liked to talk to them a bit. But they were taciturn, they wouldn't spare the time; they just got on with their job.

"Here," they said, pointing. "We can go through this gateway."

WHITE IS NOT A COLOUR. In art the white surfaces are there just to support or transport the real colours. They have no fixed quality or content in themselves. White can mean anything. I lay for a long time, perhaps an hour or so, with my eyes half open, looking at the white ceiling and blinking at the white light being reflected from the walls, before I finally asked: "Where am I?"

I could have been absolutely anywhere.

I had to ask three times before a female voice answered: "Just a minute, I'll get the doctor."

But before he finally got there, I had taken the problem in hand, as it were, and worked out the answer myself.

"You've had a little accident," he said, after he'd introduced himself.

"Yes," I said. "I know."

"You've lost a hand."

"Yes," I said. "I know that too."

"It was remarkably neatly done," he went on. "A perfect amputation. And a tourniquet. If it hadn't been for the tourniquet you wouldn't be here now."

"Yes," I said. "I'm surprised myself. And grateful."

"Is the pain bad?" he asked.

"No," I replied. "I can't feel any pain."

It was true. It is my hope that there should be no pain at all in the whole of this account. If I felt anything in my arm, it was sorrow.

"We let you sleep," he said. "And we've given you blood."

"That was kind of you," I said. "It's more than I deserve."

"There are wonderful artificial limbs nowadays," he said. "You'll be amazed. Like real hands."

137

"Yes," I said. "I've seen them. On TV."

One of the greatest American Neo-Expressionists lost both his hands in the war against Iraq a few years ago; I saw a report on his artificial hands and his sensitive painting. "It actually feels as if I've just got gloves on," he said.

I've got an artificial hand like that now. It really is a miracle, almost as if made of flesh and blood. It can move its fingers, and it can even be used for making love. But it can't write, so I have to do that with my left hand. Writing is something that can only be done by a living organism.

The doctor said there was a policeman sitting in the corridor waiting for me to wake up.

"That was considerate of him," I said.

The policeman was very young, with long hair and a fringe and a little silver ring in one ear, and a tape recorder in his hand.

"Do you feel up to it?" he asked.

"Yes, certainly," I replied.

When he'd sat down, I addressed the tape-recorder:

"It was my own fault. I brought it all on myself."

But that wasn't enough, I had to tell everything I knew about myself and what had happened to me. Who my next-of-kin was, for instance.

The only one I could think of was Paula.

At that the policeman stopped the tape.

"This is a criminal investigation," he said. "All compulsive liars babble on about knowing famous people. We must stick to the truth."

It must have taken a good half-hour for me to explain to him that my Paula was the real true Paula and not the one he knew. And obviously admired.

"She's bigger than Annie Lennox," he said. "And Madonna. And Sargonia. And Sinead O'Connor."

By the time I'd finished my explanation about Paula and how it came about that she was my only relative, so to speak, I'd more or less told him everything. But I didn't mention that I'd lost the first Madonna; I didn't want to complicate the investigation for him.

And after what had happened it also seemed to me that the second Madonna was at least as genuine as the first.

"I think I might have heard something about that painting," he said.

"I'm sure you have," I answered. "She's the most remarkable work in the whole history of Swedish art."

"Hell's bells," he said. "And you own that painting?"

I don't think I replied to that. But I told him that I didn't wish those bodyguards any harm, the two men I'd thought were bodyguards. It was all probably a ridiculous misunderstanding, there was no reason to hunt them down. They'd had a job to do, they only did what they had to. Nobody could be blamed for not knowing that the case was made the way it was and that the chain couldn't be cut with metal cutters.

"We have hundreds of reports of bags being stolen every day," he said. "We don't even try to classify them any longer. Of course this time it happened to involve a hand as well. But I don't think you need worry about them."

As he was going out he turned and said: "We'll do our utmost, I promise." I didn't ask what he meant.

Then Paula came. She cried. She had no make-up on. I tried to console her but I wasn't any good at it. She'd brought a bunch of roses. She thought everything was her fault, she'd cajoled me into this mess – she'd never be able to forgive herself. There was no order to our conversation, and in the end I was crying too, I couldn't think of any other appropriate response. She was the only one who thought of the hand itself – shouldn't it be buried? I started to say how ridiculous it would look, a little coffin with just a hand in it; the Church didn't bury separate parts of the body, only whole individuals. And we both laughed together for a few moments while the tears continued to flow.

When she'd gone I tried to sleep. But a journalist from one of the evening papers came and woke me. He'd had a tip-off. And been to the archives – or rather, the computer. "This," he said, "is an exceptional story."

"How did you get in here?" I asked. "I'm not supposed to have visitors. I might easily be dying."

"Just a couple of pictures," he said. "You holding up your maimed arm. And a few brief questions. Nothing difficult or upsetting."

He had a photographer waiting outside in the corridor, he added.

"You can go to hell," I said.

But he didn't understand me. And he objected to my choice of words.

"It doesn't fit your role to speak like that," he said. "I can't write that you swore at me. It would give a false, distorted picture of you."

"My role?"

"Can't you see for yourself," he said, "that you're going steadily downhill? Little by little you're losing everything. Your most valuable paintings, your fortune, everything you own. And now this hand. We journalists are aesthetes. It's the aesthetics of events and people's roles in them that lead us on and sell papers. There's an unpretentious tragic beauty in your life. That's what I'm trying to get at."

"I see."

"And your battle against the authorities," he went on. "And these bag-snatchers. And your friendship with Paula."

As I pressed the bell-push by my bed I said: "I'm not fighting against anyone, least of all the authorities. I've never seen any bag-snatchers. And I don't know this Paula."

It took two nurses to push him out. Whether he wrote anything about me, I have no idea.

Much more must have happened in those few days. But I've forgotten it all. The only unchanging aspect of this account is forgetfulness. I actually know an enormous amount more than I write. I forget to write it. And the more I write, the more I forget. The events around me became increasingly difficult and absurd. But that may not be apparent from my story. Instances of memory loss and oversight are increasing. I would also rather forget the next twenty pages. The end could come at any time. Paula once said that everything you forget ends up between the lines. I don't know.

She brought me my books. Or rather, the bodyguard did. She stayed in the car, she couldn't face seeing me within an hour of going on stage. It was her last performance in Stockholm before her big tour.

That's something I'd forgotten to mention: it was already May.

Another policeman came, an older, more heavily built man who called himself an inspector.

"What was it you actually had in that case?" he asked.

"*The Madonna with the Dagger*," I said. "The most exceptional of all Nils Dardel's paintings. A triptych. Folded."

"We've investigated that," he said. "It doesn't hold up."

"She's also hanging in the local magistrate's office," I said. "Back home."

"I see," he said. "Well, I'll be damned."

"There are two copies of her," I explained. "She's unique in that respect too. She's two and yet only one. A bit like the Trinity."

"So that's it," he said. "We were rather wondering."

He smiled at me. He probably wanted to show that he could see through me, he was used to fraudsters. The fact that I'd lost a hand was quite natural, it was a trick, it was part of the process of deception.

"Are you thinking of involving your insurance company?" he asked.

"The one hanging in the magistrate's office is insured," I said. "But not this one."

"How do you know which is which?" he asked.

"I can never be absolutely sure," I replied. "But I think I have a feeling for her that no one else has."

"You were up to something," he said. "It was a bit of really smart business you were planning."

"I simply wanted to have her," I said. "No one was going to be able to take her away from me. Without her my life is banal and meaningless."

He looked at me long and hard; it seemed as if he was trying to remember something he'd heard about a long time ago, and his smile gradually faded.

But then he went on: "I have a feeling that we're never going to get to the bottom of this. Some crimes solve themselves, with others we're powerless. And you should probably be grateful for that. But we'll be keeping an eye on you."

I lay in that hospital bed for five days. A couple of ribs were broken, and I'd been hit about the head. They wanted to keep me in under observation. That's what they said. I was happy there, I wasn't in a hurry to get out, I had no reason to want to be elsewhere.

When I was discharged from the hospital I couldn't go back to Paula, since she was no longer in Stockholm – her summer tour began that same evening.

I bought *Svenska Dagbladet* at Stockholm Central Station, because I didn't want to read about Paula. *Svenska Dagbladet* is the only serious newspaper in Sweden.

It was hard to hold it with only one hand: I had to use my mouth to help. The train was lurching, and the pages fell out one after another. There was an article about Paula on the arts pages, written by a sociologist of religion at the University of Lund. I was a slow reader, and the train was at Hallsberg by the time I'd got through it. I hoped that Paula wouldn't see it. It included almost everything that she probably already knew about herself. I tore out the last paragraph and folded it up and put it in my wallet:

"Whereas the dreams and images of religion have been drained of all content and dispersed like wisps of smoke or fog, and the Church, or churches, have been transubstantiated into petrified vessels holding an echoing void, the sense of a cultic community has – miraculously, perhaps even sinisterly – endured. In the centre of the new cult is the star, the image, the mass-media idol; she – for the moment in our case she, Paula (next time the name and sex will be different) – fulfils the function of priest, but is simultaneously totem animal and votive idol; she enters into proxy ecstasy, she performs the Mass. But this cultic drama no longer links man with the divine; it is a ritual pattern without aim or purpose (although possibly the battle with the beast of chaos, Tiamat, can be discerned in the obscene gestures), it is pure subjectivity, it does not point the way towards redemption or perfection. There is no liberating transcendence, no spiritual experience which can live on in us in sublimated form as memory or sympathetic relic. In the end there remains to us only one instrument in the search for redemption and catharsis: the sacrifice. Then the idol or star is slaughtered, that is the last service she performs for us; in the repulsive and blood-drenched rites of the ceremonial sacrifice she fulfils and completes the Dionysian game. Wretched stars and idols! Wretched Paula!"

Somewhere, perhaps in Mjölby or Katrineholm, my train passed another one, and Paula's mother was on it. But I didn't know that, I couldn't even imagine that she would ever again travel further than the bus station or the post office. She was on her way to an adventure that would later be much discussed and written about. She was elated, perhaps a little drunk, probably too excited to sit still in her seat, scurrying aimlessly and anxiously backwards and forwards through the carriages. I've borrowed the word "adventure" from one of the evening papers.

S HE HAD received *Swedish Women's Weekly* by post that morning. In the bathroom she read the report about Paula and her father; she'd begun storing newspapers and magazines in the bath. She was so astonished that she couldn't even bring herself to cry.

After staring at the text and photographs for almost an hour, she picked up a pair of scissors and cut out the picture of Paula whisking something in a bowl and her father standing at the cooker stirring food in a frying pan. Then she put it up on the kitchen wall with a drawing pin.

The rest of what she did that day has been described in detail in the newspapers. Everyone remembers it. And I don't know any more than that, perhaps even less. Journalists' interpretations are always richer and fuller than ordinary people's.

There was a lot she was said to have done. I think I know what she didn't do.

She didn't go to the police to seek help in getting her husband back now that she'd found him again in a magazine. She didn't put up a sign on her door to say that the music shop would cease trading or that it was for sale. It would have been superfluous anyway, since hardly anyone remembered by now that there was a music business in the house. She didn't ring Crackshot to get a free ticket for Paula's first concert in Västerås. She didn't write a dramatic letter to Paula. She didn't give me her keys. As she left I had just got on the train in Stockholm.

She put a salt herring in to soak for the next day. Then she dressed herself in patched jeans and a washed-out denim jacket, tied a fiery red scarf round her neck and fastened a broad black belt round her waist to which she attached a copper brooch, a bust of Beethoven. She put rouge on her cheeks and crimson lipstick on her lips and violet-blue eye shadow on her eyes. Finally she drew on her big black wig which had lain in a drawer with all her stockings and blouses and tights that were waiting to be washed and mended, rubbed in hair gel, raked her fingers through it and sprayed it till it stood on end like a tangled and straggling plume around her chubby excited face.

She hid her keys in the flower basket that hung from the roof of the verandah, under the flower pot with the dead fuchsia in it.

She had taken a book with her to read on the train. *The Dream Within*, by Barbara Cartland. When she got off the bus at the railway station she left it in the luggage rack by mistake.

She had a bottle of sweet vermouth in her bag. And sunglasses. And a little tape recorder to record Paula's concert.

She'd never been to Västerås before. How she found her way to the Municipal Park I have no idea. She must have asked one of the local bus drivers.

She was one of the first at the entrance gate; she probably got there by four o'clock. She'd put her sunglasses on. If she'd kept her place in the queue she was in she would have been one of the lucky ones nearest to the stage; she might even have been the one to catch the gold-embroidered blouse or skirt that Paula threw out into the audience at the end of the first number. But every so often she gave up her place to someone else, moving back through the queue, deliberately and methodically, as if her intention was to be one of the countless number in the middle, neither first nor last, but one of the crowd, anonymous among the humbly adoring fans.

When the gates finally opened she had achieved what she had presumably been aiming at; she was lifted and propelled forward by forces that she couldn't control, forces that represented a concentrate of rapture and devotion, worship and adoration in its purest form; and she was just an anonymous and insignificant constituent of an astounding record audience.

But after a while, as she was pushed and carried forward, she started involuntarily thinking, to her own surprise, about the powers that were being aroused, this distilled and roaring surge of inspiration, and she realised in a new and fundamental way that the source of this unparalleled energy was Paula. Obviously she had known that before, that was why she had come, but her superficial insight was transformed now in a few short moments into deep spiritual experience. She herself would have said that she felt it in her mother's heart.

She was filled with an intoxicating and irrepressible pride.

She braced her hands and knees against the bodies nearest to her, and fought for a little room for manoeuvre so that she could turn round and face the sea of people surging forward behind her. She raised herself on tiptoe, she even tried to climb on to a stocky muscular youth who had ended up next to her, and finally she tore off her sunglasses and her grotesque wig and held them high above her head, waving them strenuously, almost desperately, as she cried out: "Can't you see who I am? I'm Paula's mother. It's me, I'm Paula's little mother."

But no one heard her, no one took any notice of her, and as she had turned right round and was facing into the oncoming movement of the crowd she stumbled and fell backwards, and was immediately trampled into the ground. No one seemed to be aware of what was happening, and not a single witness could be found afterwards.

That is more or less how I imagine it went.

I knew nothing, of course. Nor did Paula.

That evening was one of the biggest and most spectacular in her life.

Her bodyguards weren't able to get her out through a back door until three hours after the performance had ended, and then only with her dressed as a cleaner, with a black shawl over her head and wearing a grey full-length cloak to make her look like an immigrant.

They didn't find the remains of Paula's mother until the next morning. It was almost impossible to distinguish her from the beer cans, cigarette stubs and soiled articles of clothing. And it was afternoon by the time the police had identified her. They found her handbag kicked under the stage, the bottle of vermouth was smashed and the tape recorder stolen. A little photo of Paula and herself, and a Co-op membership card, revealed her identity.

The photograph was a forgery: I had helped her to construct it. I had cut two pictures and glued them together, I was the one who'd put her arm round Paula's shoulders and made them smile at each other by retouching their pupils. Then she'd had the photo re-photographed.

I did nothing that evening. I probably went to bed almost as soon as I got home; I didn't go down to the workshop or the shop, I read Michael Harner's *The Way of the Shaman* for a while and listened to Sven-David Sandström's "Berceuse for a Child in Baghdad" on the radio. I knew that Paula wouldn't phone.

During the morning of the next day I went round trying to teach my left hand everything it would need to know from then on. How to open doors and cupboards and pull out drawers and lift the pick-up on the record player and shuffle cards and lay out a game of patience. It was hard.

I can't give such a clear and unequivocal account of what took place in the afternoon and evening as I would wish. Sometimes two events can happen simultaneously and merge together so that both become unintelligible and unreal; they cancel each other out like a plus and a minus, and you can no longer manage to recollect either of them. Even though you take part yourself in everything that happens, you feel as if you're transposed to an indeterminate point outside the events and are just a confused spectator. I think Schopenhauer wrote about that somewhere, but I can't remember where.

First of all Paula rang. And then I had an unexpected visitor. It was all beyond my comprehension.

147

S O PAULA RANG. She was in Gävle, and would be on stage in four hours. The hotel porter had given her a note of the phone number of the Västerås police, who had been trying to contact her.

Her voice was clear and slightly dry as always; she explained plainly and succinctly what had happened. I think she was simply repeating what the police had told her. "It must have all taken place so quickly that my mother wouldn't have had time to react," she said, "she wouldn't have understood what was happening, she wouldn't have suffered."

I sat down on the floor by the telephone table. I'd actually been closer to Paula's mother than Paula herself had been. I had to dry my eyes with the bandage on my right arm.

"You must never think for a moment that it was your fault," I said.

"I don't understand what you mean," Paula replied. "How could it be my fault?"

I could hear her chewing on something. Probably a kebab. I don't think she ever ate anything except kebabs at that period.

"How will you manage?" I asked. "And then this whole tour that you'll have to cancel."

"Why should I cancel it? What's done is done. I can't let my public down. My mother would never have wanted that."

"No," I agreed. "That's true. She would have turned in her grave."

That was really the wrong thing to say, since she hadn't yet been buried. We were silent for a long time; everything seemed unreal to us and we couldn't understand it: perhaps we still haven't understood it.

Our conversation was of course much longer and fuller than it appears to be as I do my best now to recall it and write it down. It's possible that the same applies to all the conversations I've tried to reconstruct. I summarise them, and they become stylised, rather like landscapes by Rousseau, or even Feininger.

"I wish you weren't on your own," I said. "And you must be careful with all those pills and concoctions."

It was hardly necessary to say that, since Paula never even took aspirin.

"I'm not on my own," she replied. "He'll be with me. For a whole week."

She called him by name of course, but I can't do so here, because he's still actively practising in Stockholm and in his private clinic in the country. It would be cruel to expose him, her plastic surgeon. I also talked about him as if I'd known him for ages. He'd taken time off from his work and family to be with her. The journalists never discovered that.

This was at the very time when the newspapers were writing about her forthcoming marriage with a Norwegian shipowner.

I said that was perfect, that was just what she needed, and I felt relieved immediately. "Will you be coming back home here?" I asked.

She would never come back home, an estate agent would be selling everything, she never wanted to see the house and the furniture and the musical instruments again. Right now she would really like an arsonist to take pity on her and set fire to everything she would inherit.

At that we both burst out laughing. But only in a rather fleeting and unnatural manner.

Then she asked me to go over to the music shop and see whether anything needed doing, whether there were any taps running or the cooker left on. She told me to look round and see whether there was anything I wanted: I could take whatever I liked, she was sure that was exactly what her mother would have wished. For

God's sake, if it would be any good to me I could gladly have the whole house.

"Thanks," I said. "But I have far more than I need already."

Before we finished Paula said: "I was bloody good yesterday. It was a shame my mother couldn't have heard me. I'm better than I've ever been."

I had the impression that her voice sounded momentarily slightly shrill and uncertain.

"Can't there still be any chance of a mistake?" I asked. "Some kind of mix-up?"

"No," Paula replied. "Her personal identity number was on her dentures."

I forgot to mention that a page or two back when I was describing how the police identified Paula's mother. There's a law about identity numbers on dentures.

"I ought to have realised that this was exactly what had to happen to her," said Paula.

When I got up and looked out of the window I could see that the bedside light was on in her bedroom. She had obviously thought that it might be night-time and dark by the time she got back home.

"It will be terribly empty without her," I said. In a way, that was absolutely true.

Then I stood at the window for a long time looking at her house. All the venetian blinds were broken and hanging askew, the plaster had fallen off round the shop door and on the corners of the house, the gutters had rusted through and come loose in various places, and the neon light showed only M and c: the U S I had gone out several years before. She always said how much she loved that house. One fine day she would astonish us all and renovate everything – she would face it with white weather-boarding and build an entrance porch with white pillars and put a clock-tower on the roof. For the time being she was just keeping it going; she wanted it to be like an antique ornament.

I had no desire ever to go in there again; I wished it could stand undisturbed and boarded up and carry on decaying in the same way it had done up to now. In a few years it would fall into ruin of its own accord and rot away.

I had to fetch a chair to stand on so that my clumsy left hand could pick up the key that was hidden in its usual place, beneath the dead fuchsia in the hanging basket on the verandah.

I hadn't been in there for several weeks. Everything seemed to have changed and become alien in a way that's hard to explain. But I gradually realised that it had always looked like that – what had happened was that Paula's mother had disappeared, she no longer stood in the way and ran around catching my eye with her gestures and cries and motley clothes, and she didn't sit down at the piano and force me to watch her while she did her finger exercises.

The walls were covered from floor to ceiling with record sleeves and posters and press cuttings, placards that she'd stolen from outside newsagents, and magazine covers, and I couldn't see even the tiniest glimpse of wallpaper or paint.

Paula, everywhere Paula.

But there were a few others here and there: a princess in Monaco, a racing driver, a young Kennedy in the U.S.A. suspected of possessing drugs, two opera singers talking about their lesbian love, John Travolta, Ingmar Bergman. As if she'd wanted to say: Paula isn't entirely alone, there are others of the same kind, the absolute and the incomparable can take many forms, a monumental life is always mysterious and exposed.

I stopped for a moment in the kitchen in front of the photograph of Paula and her father posing with the empty bowl and pan – it really looked as if they were preparing food together, and despite the fact that I'd been standing there watching and knew how false and prearranged the picture was, I couldn't help believing in it. And I had a feeling that I was still there myself, though invisible.

There were no taps running or dripping, the cooker was cold, the plug on the iron pulled out. I wandered through the cluttered rooms looking at the furniture and the ornaments, porcelain ballet dancers and woven baskets, brass candlesticks and coloured glass bowls, table lamps made from old liqueur bottles and a bronze plaque bearing the words YOUTH MUSIC FESTIVAL SKÖVDE 1975. The music for "Sleep in My Arms" was lying with the guitar on the plush sofa by the piano. That was where I used to sit when Paula had her first piano lessons. There were piles of magazines lying on all the tables and chairs and on every inch of spare floor space.

Paula had told me to take something away with me, anything at all, anything I would like to have, I could pick out whatever I wanted. In the end I went back to the kitchen and took the herring that had been left to soak.

When I got home again I discovered I had a visitor, standing at the back door. He had a large package in his arms. It was Gulliver.

I was holding the herring by its tail in my one hand, so I couldn't shake hands.

"I'm not making any more frames," I said. "The picture-frame business is closed. I can't hold the tools any more."

I waved my maimed arm up and down a little. I thought he'd brought something he'd found at auction for framing.

"But maybe if you got an artificial hand?" he said. "They make wonderful artificial limbs nowadays."

"No," I replied. "I'll think of something else. There's any number of possibilities."

He followed me inside. I could hear him puffing and panting behind me as I went up the stairs. The package he was carrying was wrapped in brown paper. I put the herring on the draining board.

"It was devilish bad luck, that was," he said. "You'd never think such a thing could happen."

The papers must have already reported the news about Paula's mother.

"In some ways we're all responsible ourselves for the accidents that befall us," I said. "You have to lie low. As soon as you go out of the door anything can happen to you."

"We never thought it would turn out like that," he went on. "We didn't want there to be any violence. Or at most so little that it would never be noticed."

I couldn't understand what he could have to do with the accident in Västerås. Was he connected with music and artistes too? Like Uncle Erland?

"We?" I said. "What we?"

"We in the consortium," he replied. "We hired those two boys. They were doing the job for us."

That was when I began to realise he wasn't talking about Paula's mother at all.

He looked wretched; he was holding up the package as if he was trying to hide behind it – I think I even remember him having tears in his eyes.

"I see," I said. "That's something I didn't know. That you can buy those kinds of services."

"Anything can be fixed up," said Gulliver. "If you ever need help with something, just say. I have contacts. Then you'll be O.K."

"Thanks," I said. "I'll remember."

"Though it costs, of course. But if you've got a consortium behind you, you can manage most things."

We'd sat down in armchairs in the living room, and he'd laid the package on the table between us. My fingers reeked of herring.

"I've got everything a person could need," I said. "And I'd be no use in a consortium."

"Anyway, as I said, it wasn't our intention," he said. "This business of your hand. They were rather too extreme, so to speak, those boys."

He was sweating profusely, and kept wiping his face on the sleeve of his jacket.

"Extremists are always a risk," I said. "You can never be sure of them."

But I went on to add: "I've only myself to blame. It was an idiotic idea, the case and chain."

"No, it was a good thought," said Gulliver. "You can never be too careful. I'd have probably done the same in your shoes. Security never comes cheap."

"I shouldn't have gone out," I said. "I should have stayed in the apartment. Everything was perfect, I wouldn't have wanted for anything."

"It wouldn't have helped," he said. "The boys were keeping watch outside. They would have gone in to get her. Once they've got their orders, they never give up."

I sat thinking that I ought to cook the herring. As soon as I'd got rid of him I'd peel three potatoes and cut up an onion.

"A hand isn't the whole world," I remarked. "Even if Heidegger said it was."

"Heidegger?"

"He was German," I replied. "A philosopher. He said that it's hands that make us human."

He was silent for a moment. I think he was wondering whether to pretend he knew who Heidegger was.

"It's all the fault of the authorities really," he continued. "If they hadn't said you would be getting her back. In the newspapers."

"The authorities do their best," I said. "They're no worse than other people."

"We thought you'd got her straight away. That you'd taken her with you to Stockholm."

"Of course," I said. "I'm not blaming you. That was the most likely thing."

"This has been a great torment for me," he went on. "It's been constantly weighing on my mind and pricking my conscience. I haven't been able to sleep at night."

The bags under his eyes were even more swollen than before and he was blinking incessantly. He certainly did look as if he'd been having sleepless nights.

"You don't need to worry for my sake," I said. "And you're not responsible for anything. You're not guilty. It was an accident, that's all."

154

"Won't you open the package?" he asked.

He pushed it towards me so that it almost fell into my lap.

"For God's sake," I said. "I shouldn't get anything. I've done nothing to deserve presents."

But nevertheless I picked up the little knife from the table and cut the strings.

"We took a vote," said Gulliver. "In the consortium. And we were completely unanimous."

There were layers of newspapers under the brown wrapping paper. And inside all the papers was the Madonna.

I can't remember saying anything. I just stared at the lustrous panels, it didn't even occur to me to open out the side pieces to stand her up. In the slanting light from the window behind us the first owner's initials showed up clearly, the W.G. that he'd scratched into the wood with a darning needle on the railway station in Verdun.

"It's only right and proper," said Gulliver. "You're the one who should have her. If we can give real pleasure to our fellow human beings, then we shouldn't hesitate, for heaven's sake."

At that instant the telephone rang.

"Excuse me," I said, "but I'll have to answer it. We can continue this ceremony afterwards."

I really felt that it was a ceremony.

It was Paula again. This time she sounded in despair; her voice kept breaking again and again.

At first I couldn't understand what it was that had upset her, I thought it must be grief that had suddenly struck belatedly, but then I realised it was the funeral she was talking about. Perhaps I wasn't listening properly – my thoughts were still on the Madonna. And Gulliver.

Uncle Erland had arrived in Gävle. He'd driven from Stockholm to Gävle in less than two hours. He wanted the funeral to be one of the most impressive and grandiose events of the decade, this very exclusive death in such exceptional circumstances – a chance like this wasn't to be missed. This was a case where you could really call death a gift from the gods. He'd already arranged things with the only festival organiser of real genius in Sweden, a man called Michael Bindefeld.

"What did you say his name was?" I asked.

She repeated it: "Michael Bindefeld."

He'd talked about having the service in Stockholm Cathedral and an ensemble from the Royal Orchestra and the Dean or maybe even the Bishop, a sea of irises and roses and lilies, and a Wagnerian soprano to sing "*Starke Scheite*" from the *Götterdämmerung*, and two or at most three speeches on the subject of mother/art/sacrifice, and a three-quarter-hour march-past, and a gigantic supper afterwards for two hundred people in the banqueting suite of the Royal Opera House Restaurant.

I interrupted Paula when she began stuttering and crying and snuffling and could hardly get her words out any more.

"Nobody else knew her," I said. "Not as we did. We're the ones who should bury her. Just us two."

Paula quietened down.

"You and I will arrange it all," I went on. "It's not the first funeral in my life and he needn't think we're dependent on him. We'll manage it. What she deserves is just an ordinary decent burial, nothing more."

"I hoped that was what you'd say," Paula replied. "But I didn't dare believe it."

"There's no question about it," I said. "It's the least we can do for her."

"Shall I say that to Uncle Erland?"

"You can not only say it, you must drum it into his head. He should keep his hands off everything to do with your mother, he didn't own her and he can give up any damned ideas of trying to exploit her now."

We agreed that I should go to Stockholm to make all the necessary arrangements. I still had a key to her apartment. Paula would phone me from time to time so that we could agree on all the details as we went along. We would devise a suitable and fitting funeral. Or to put it another way: the only proper funeral for a person such as Paula's mother.

When I came back to Gulliver he looked as if he'd fallen asleep, but as I sat down he opened his eyes and looked up at me, in a slightly sad but also kindly manner.

"And she was just a fake anyway," he said. "A devilishly convincing one, it has to be said, but pure fraud nevertheless."

"How dare you?" I protested. "How the hell can you presume to say that?"

I was still thinking of Paula's mother. And the funeral.

"We got an expert to look at her," Gulliver replied. "And he said that she was certainly a masterpiece, but a forgery all the bloody same."

I realised then that he meant the Madonna.

"And we in the consortium are honourable people," he continued. "We don't want to put any forged paintings on to the market."

"I see," I said. "An expert."

"I don't know him myself," said Gulliver. "It was the boys in Stockholm who went to him. But he's said to know more than anyone else. About genuine and false."

"He made a mistake this time," I said. "No painting could be more genuine than this one."

"You can talk to him yourself," said Gulliver. "I can get his name for you. They called him Goatee. He lives on Döbelnsgatan, I know that much."

"There's no need," I replied. "I know she's genuine. And that's enough for me."

"The genuine one is still hanging in the local magistrate's office," said Gulliver.

"Yes," I said. "She's genuine too."

Before leaving he said: "We thought you'd be grateful. But you're as hard as nails. We've actually gone to a hell of a lot of trouble for your sake. You tried to pull the wool over our eyes. We could have been upset and angry. But we turned the other cheek. You bastard."

*

When at last I was on my own again, I unfolded the Madonna and set her up on the arms of the chair that he'd been sitting in. Nothing had happened to her, the paint was clean and undamaged, she had no scratches or tears. The consortium and the boys and Gulliver had handled her as lovingly as I would have done myself. With the help of my magnifying-glass I found the little crimson dot straight away, Goatee's signature. I could even see it as I sat in my armchair, without the magnifying-glass. And I could still see it when I got up and went over to the door if I looked really carefully. The little spot of colour hadn't changed, it was as insignificant as before, but my eyes were now suddenly able to pick it out so that it glowed and burned like a microscopic Bengal light. I was astonished.

After I'd cooked the herring and eaten it I folded up the Madonna again and pushed her under the bed. Then I lay awake half the night trying to devise a worthy and beautiful funeral for Paula's mother – no, not one, but a hundred possible funerals: I wanted Paula to be able to choose the one she'd really like most of all.

W<small>E CHOSE</small> Church-in-the-Wood. Paula had three days free between Umeå and Karlstad, Tuesday, Wednesday and Thursday, two weeks after the accident in Västerås. She and the plastic surgeon had actually been going to fly to Paris, but now there had to be a funeral instead.

The coffin was mahogany, with straight sides and a flat lid. It looked rather like a large document chest from the Renaissance, that might contain almost anything. There were carved hop tendrils on the lid and the ends, the flower of escapism and innocence.

As for living flowers, we'd ordered just white roses and lilies. A minister from the Missionary Society officiated – we'd found his name in the telephone book. He had a loud squeaky voice and was permanently red with excitement. He told us himself that this was the most memorable ceremony of his life. There were no speeches. Two students from the National School of Drama read poems: Leopardi's "Setting of the Moon" and Claudel's "Virgin at Noon". It was Paula who had chosen the poems.

One of her guitarists had recorded "Sleep in My Arms", and Paula Music Studios had made a two-hour version; the loudspeakers were hidden behind the flower arrangements.

Paula was on her own – though actually she wasn't: I walked by her side and sat with her. But there was nobody to support her or to hold her hand. I walked on her left, and couldn't bring myself to hold out my artificial hand; she probably wouldn't have wanted to hold it or squeeze it in any case.

That's something I'd forgotten to mention: I got my artificial hand the day before the funeral. It was a temporary one, but even so quite well done. The hand had nails and veins and was slightly hairy, and it could grip and hold things.

But we hadn't succeeded in keeping Crackshot out entirely. God knows how he contrived it, but he always found out everything he needed to know.

He had invited about a hundred people, and they all had to shake hands with Paula and say a few words of consolation. Artistes and sports stars and millionaires and lawyers and a couple of politicians and a film director and a television newsreader and Lars Forssell the author, from the Swedish Academy. I knew nobody.

He had ordered wreaths, paid for by Paula Music Ltd. One from the King and Queen. One from Princess Victoria. One from the head of the Swedish Arts Council. One from the editor of *The Express*. And an enormous arrangement of ferns from the Fredrika Bremer Society. You could easily have thought it was Paula herself and not just her mother who was being buried.

And he'd granted sole rights in the funeral to *Swedish Women's Weekly*.

That's how it came about that the only significant event to occur was so fully photographed and reported and became so widely known.

Paula cried throughout the whole ceremony, silently and inwardly, drying her eyes with a handkerchief from time to time. And I could see her hands trembling.

But when we had to step forward as the first to lay our white roses on the lid of the coffin, she could control herself no longer; her whole body started shaking and she almost collapsed, so I had to put my arm around her and support her and guide her. And as we stood staring at the coffin with our heads bowed, as one should, the tears came streaming out of her, and no longer in silence. No one could hear "Sleep in My Arms" any more, she was shouting out her grief, she was screaming for her mother so sickeningly and deafeningly that I could see the people sitting nearest discreetly putting their hands over their ears. Everyone knows that Paula's voice is one of the strongest in Sweden.

I didn't know what to do; I tried stroking her back with my artificial hand but it didn't seem to help.

Suddenly I noticed someone running towards us, someone who had been sitting a long way back in the hall, zig-zagging through the rows of seats with his jacket flapping and his hair flying, and when he got to us he simply took Paula in his arms, patted her head and stroked her cheek, and muttered and whispered something I couldn't hear. Paula fell silent. The shaking continued for a few moments and when he let go of her she hid her face in her hands, but the noisy sobs had stopped.

The pictures appeared in *Swedish Women's Weekly* and eventually in all the other magazines and newspapers with the caption "Paula's Doctor".

So that was the plastic surgeon. I'd never seen him before. He didn't look as I'd expected. We were standing next to one another for some time. You could see the way I was looking at him on the photographs. Penetratingly, one of the journalists should have written.

He was shorter than I was and had dark hair, combed back, dark bushy eyebrows, big lips that were so red that you'd think he had lipstick on, and a little dimple in his chin. He resembled Klaus Mann in Dardel's drawing. Though a much older Klaus Mann, of course. But we exchanged not a single word.

When we turned, Paula and I, and walked off slowly down the aisle, he followed behind, but somewhere along the way he went off to one side and hid himself among the celebrities. He wasn't to be seen on the photographs, it was only Paula and myself, she leaning against me, and it looked as if she had put her hand under my arm.

We didn't take any notice of all those guests we hadn't invited. I don't know what they did after we disappeared, perhaps they stayed sitting there for a while listening to "Sleep in My Arms". We went straight to Church-in-the-Wood station and took the underground back to the centre of Stockholm. A squirrel followed us right up to the platform barrier.

Then we found a little Italian restaurant on Apelbergsgatan.

Nobody there knew Paula, and we could be left in peace. Not even the bodyguard was with us – that's how Paula had wanted it and for once she'd got her own way. Paula had a pizza, I had veal cutlets. And three glasses of pure aquavit. These are the funeral meats, we said.

I sat and looked at her. She had wept all the make-up off her face. Her skin was perfectly white against her black clothes, and her features were still round like those of a child. I thought about how fresh and uncorrupted she was inside, how genuine and sound in her heart. She would never be able to do any evil. We didn't talk much. "It was a beautiful funeral," I said. "Do you think so?" Paula replied.

We said nothing about what it really was that we'd buried out there at Church-in-the-Wood. No one but we two knew, not even *Swedish Women's Weekly*. It was ten stone of *This Week*, 1988–1992.

The second burial, the real one, took place the day after, at home in our own church. Or rather, in the little chapel under the lime trees behind the bell-tower. The undertakers had collected Paula's mother from Västerås. The coffin was white with thin open-work gold palmette mouldings. It was just Paula and myself. And the vicar, the one who'd prepared me for confirmation.

He didn't use the word funeral, he said family ceremony. He took Paula by the arm and walked about with her; he showed her the organ loft in the church where she'd stood and sung Beethoven's "Ode to Joy" when she was a little girl with flaming red hair, and he took her to see the most important graves in the churchyard, two members of parliament and a professor and a famous sculptor. And so when we came to the chapel where the coffin was already lying, it seemed to be just one more element in the tour. He stopped for a while and performed the burial service.

Paula's mother was no stranger to him. He had really been her spiritual guide, she used to seek him out from time to time. We hadn't known that. She was a good person and a Christian, he said, a mother that any child in the world might have wished for. And that in the deepest sense every child deserved. Now her heart's desire has led her into Eternity, he said.

I wasn't interested in anything except Paula. Her eyes were wide open and her cheeks and chin trembling with the strain, she was doing her utmost to grieve. She'd imagined that the grief would come now, the deep genuine sorrow, that she would be able to give free rein to her despair.

But she couldn't manage it, she had no grief left, she had used it up the day before at Church-in-the-Wood.

The vicar wanted us to go in for tea and sandwiches at the vicarage. But Paula didn't have time, she had to be in Karlstad the next morning and the car we'd ordered was already waiting at the gates. We stayed for a few minutes by the grave that I'd bought and charged to Paula Music Ltd, in the south corner where the stone wall meets the fir hedge. "Everything will be fine," Paula said. There's an old pear tree in front of the stone wall. That's where Paula's mother is buried, in our banal little churchyard. In reality, so to speak.

We never bought that issue of *Swedish Women's Weekly*, the funeral issue. But we didn't escape it altogether: the magazine sold the photographs on, and the other newspapers and magazines provided their own stories. I was included in the story. I even appeared on the placards. "The new man in Paula's life." "The obscure art-dealer." "The mysterious multi-millionaire." "The childhood friend."

I had entered the scene.

So Paula went on her way, to Karlstad and Borlänge and Sundsvall, Landskrona, Bengtsfors, Växjö, Norrköping and all the other places that Uncle Erland had selected for her. I stayed at home. She rang every evening. Her tour wouldn't be over until September. Paula's victory march, the evening papers said. When I went to the shop to buy yoghurt or bread I would stop at the bus station and read the newspaper placards.

Some long time afterwards, we received a little urn from the crematorium at Church-in-the-Wood. By then several things had happened that I haven't written about yet. I was back in Stockholm. We put the urn in a plastic bag and went to Tysta gatan and emptied the ashes into a litter bin outside the editorial offices of *This Week*.

Those were long days; there was nothing for me to do. I started teaching my left hand to hold a pen. It was difficult, and everything I wrote seemed childish yet at the same time pretentious and pathetic – it was not just the letters but also the text itself that had something uncontrollably inflated about it. I don't know whether it was really the fault of the hand. When I still had both hands I hardly wrote anything.

I wrote letters that I never posted. To the authorities. And to Paula. And Crackshot. And Goatee. And Gulliver.

This is something I wrote late one evening on a piece of cardboard:

I think I can confidently state that this funeral – no, these two funerals – represented a turning-point in my life. They opened my eyes to the possibility of a new world-order, or even more than that: an unexpected freedom and security, a breast to lay my head on, a form of being that unites art and life, an existence that, put quite simply, embodies the highest and most essential and hitherto unattainable for me: pure, unfalsified art, the world as arrangement.

It was painful. I had to remind myself of who I really was: a picture-frame maker who could no longer even cut out a damned picture mounting.

Two men from an auction firm came with a lorry and emptied the music shop. And the rooms Paula's mother had lived in.

When they'd finished and were about to go, one of them came over to me with a big brown envelope.

"We can't take this," he said, handing it to me. "There's a limit to what can be sold."

I opened the envelope. There were six enlargements in it. Colour prints. She'd obviously had herself photographed in the last few months. She was wearing a deeply décolleté dress and giving a big warm smile with her mouth half open and eyes screwed up. She'd probably intended to select one of the portraits to send to Paula. But in one of them she'd forgotten she was sitting for a photographer, and her mouth had fallen open a bit further, but without a smile, her cheeks were sagging loosely and her eyes were sad and staring emptily at some indeterminate point above and below the camera.

"They're beautiful," I said. "I'll take care of them."

"We burn everything that can't be sold," he said. "But that sort of photograph is like a living person."

The new owners started moving in that same evening. They were going to live on the first floor. In the old music shop they were going to have a picture-framing workshop and sell paintings. They came to me before they bought the house. They were in their fifties and had had a glass-merchant's shop before near the town of Örebro. He had a pronounced stutter; she was the one who did most of the talking.

All he managed to say was: "Art hahas acacactually ahalways bebebeen mymymy lililife." It sounded exactly as it used to sound in my mind when I used to think the same thought.

"You seem to have closed down your business," he went on.

"It just happened that way," I replied. "The business closed itself down. I never had to make a decision about it."

They bought all that I had, tools and mouldings and workbench and the piles of packing material and the hand-painted landscapes, they even bought the FRAMES & PICTURES sign. I simply named a sum and they paid immediately. I forgot to mention that. I didn't need to think about the framing business any longer.

At this point I ought to write about everything I've forgotten that really has to be known if subsequent events and the actions of Paula and myself are to be understood. An account such as this must contain the same number of causes as effects. But it's always easier to remember an effect than a cause. Chance is perhaps no more than the sum of all the causes that we've forgotten.

I took out the black chest that had stood empty ever since I bought the Madonna, and put the money in it. It was a surprisingly large amount; it was almost painful to take it. I hadn't thought that anyone would ever want to buy anything from me again; I'd imagined that my tools and mouldings and cardboard packaging and paintings would crumble away to dust in the end – they no longer seemed to have anything to do with me.

From now on I'm not going to mention sums of money by exact amounts. I shall just write "a fairly large sum" or "a tidy little packet" or "an unbelievably large sum". At this stage of the story a little caution and discretion begin to be necessary. I don't want to harm or offend anyone.

I sent the envelope containing the photographs of Paula's mother to the City Hotel in Karlskrona, where she would be in two days' time.

I shouldn't have done that.

Or: It was lucky I did that.

I don't know.

I had written a little note of greeting and explained what the pictures were. Paula sat staring at them for a long time. Some day in the future she would look like that that woman. The thought pleased her. There was after all a kind of peace in that face. Or a confused yet intelligent resignation.

Then she put them on top of a suitcase. She didn't know what to do with them. Perhaps she could ask the cleaner to take them and burn them.

That was where Uncle Erland found them. He'd come down to Karlskrona to reassure himself that all was well with Paula. He'd also brought five rabbits.

I'll explain in a moment what the rabbits were for. Even though most people must have seen it and remember it.

He examined the photographs one by one. He hadn't seen Paula's mother for several years, and he probably felt a slight sadness. Then he was inspired with a grandiose idea. When he left he took the pictures with him.

That same evening, in Karlskrona, mother and daughter appeared together on stage. The photographs of Paula's mother were projected on to a screen twenty feet high and twelve feet wide, first the five smiling pictures and finally the relaxed melancholy one – she was present, as it were, for the whole performance. Her date of death had been printed in black ink above her bouffant hair.

It's hard to describe how those giant faces in the background affected the performance as a whole. Enough to say, as Uncle Erland did: "It was devilishly effective."

The audience recognised her immediately: her pictures had been in all the newspapers and on television after the accident in Västerås. Many of them even shouted out at the very moment the projector was switched on: "Paula's Mum!" As the pictures changed and faded into one another the eyes and lips seemed to move. It looked as if she'd been hastily and fleetingly brought back to life to join in Paula's singing. The whole thing was an astonishing and poignant meeting between mother and daughter, between two widely differing types of womanhood: one half withered and exhausted and the other explosively blossoming and vital. But it also constituted a meeting between life and death, between the

167

principles of birth and of destruction. It was especially manifest in Paula's final number, the song called "The Orpheus Number".

I hardly need to describe it, of course.

Paula was one of the maenads, her dress consisted of a few scraps of cloth hanging over her shoulders and round her waist, and the music was described in one of the national dailies as follows: "The rhythms and riffs create a heady and monotonous clash, this is a meeting of machines, a lacerated yet crystal-clear voice and squealing guitars in an abandoned homage to emotion; into over-drive for the intoxicating rush of speed. This is the most powerful torment in Sweden."

I think the whole number was based on a poem by Hjalmar Gullberg. In the text of the poem the god's women appear in the light of smoking torches with a singing head, its eyes extinguished, drifting out to sea; they had slit him open like a goat and drunkenly slurped up his blood. "And to the hounds his genitals" – I remember that word for word. As a finale, while the guitars screamed and wailed in a violent and extended crescendo, Orpheus would be slaughtered and sacrificed.

And that was where the rabbits came in.

Of course it should really have been a well-built young man, an athletic dancer. But that kind of thing was simply not possible. So it had to be a rabbit instead.

It would be crouching, tied by a cord to a ring in the floor of the stage. Paula would snip the cord and lift up the rabbit and stroke it, and then cut off its head. She had practised doing it with a single cut, and the blood would spurt out of the Orpheus-rabbit. The people who forced their way to the front seats would struggle to catch a few drops on their clothes; a jacket or pair of jeans with spots of the blood on could be sold for thousands of crowns.

And now Uncle Erland and the choreographer had come up with a little addition to this number that highlighted the elements of pubescence and infantile immaturity it already contained. Paula danced to the back of the stage with her hand pressed tightly over the rabbit's severed neck, and when she was almost up to the screen on which her mother's face glowed and shimmered she swung quickly round and sprayed as much blood as she could on to the projected picture. It was that unfortunate, melancholy photograph. Paula's mother staring out into empty space. It looked exactly as if she were mourning her own death.

It's impossible to say what that final addition was actually supposed to signify. Ancient myths can be put to almost any use, and people just have a vague feeling that they conceal some kind of meaning. Or several different meanings. No one can ever be certain.

Nor do I know whether the gigantic screen with the photograph of Paula's mother was actually successful. It emphasised the bold and challenging nature of Paula's art. And the puerile. No one could help being moved by it. She also continued to break one audience attendance record after another. Though it's hard to say how an audience record comes about, since the record belongs to the audience, as the audience's own little secret.

So she used one rabbit each evening. Uncle Erland got them for her.

Paula phoned after the performance in Karlskrona and told me what she was being forced to do now, on top of everything else. She was crying.

"Do you want me to come?" I asked. "I've got nothing else to do. I'm playing patience, that's all."

"No," she replied. "I don't want you around as well. That would only make things worse."

I think she meant that that would involve even more of her private life, the part that was really her, in this artificial, false world. She really wanted to be a professional. She had a deep and genuine respect for her own artistry. The newspapers said so too.

As I sat there playing patience I was listening to the radio. That was how I heard of Uncle Erland's death.

An accident. In Linköping. Fifty-eight years old. Businessman and manager, impresario, the man who had created countless numbers of artistes, but first and foremost Paula. It was four o'clock.

I was so shocked that I counted wrong as I was setting out the cards. I had to shuffle the pack five times before the patience was set out as it should be.

News often upsets and confuses me. When I've read or heard an item of news I immediately know much less than I did before.

Now she must need me, I thought.

The patience wouldn't come out. It never does.

When I tried putting the pack of cards into the palm of my artificial hand the cards slipped down and spread themselves all over the floor. I'd drunk half a bottle of aquavit. I went to pick them up, tipped the chair over, fell into the bookshelves and ended up lying under piles of art books. I fell asleep with my head on *Dreams Beneath an Arctic Sky*.

But not even sleep could prevent me thinking over and over again: Now it's me she needs, no one else has the necessary strength and resilience. Now I shall definitely have to take care of her.

T HEN PAULA phoned. I managed to answer it after the fifth ring.

She told me in calm and simple words about Uncle Erland. There was no sorrow or agitation in her voice; she said nothing about how close they'd been to each other. She was staying at the Freemasons Hotel. On the third floor. He had brought the photographs she had to sign for the Paula Fan Club, a bursting suit-case full. And some songs for her to look at. And a new batch of rabbits.

They'd talked about one of the lyrics. The title was "Hot Flesh and Blood Sandwiches of Eternity".

"Do you really have to write on all those cards yourself?" I asked. "Couldn't you have a signature stamp?"

"Everything has to be genuine," Paula replied. "Otherwise I don't want anything to do with it."

Suddenly, he had thrown himself out of the window, just straight out. She didn't understand. The final words he spoke were: "You're going to be the greatest in the whole world, Paula." He lost one shoe as he made that terrible leap, and she remembered standing after-wards with the shoe in her hand, reading over and over again in her bewilderment the word "Aristocrat" imprinted in the sole. She heard the ambulance come and the noise and the screams of the crowd that had gathered, but she didn't think of going down, she didn't even look out of the window.

"It's a Swedish make," I said. "Aristocrat. Much more comfortable than Italian ones."

Then the police came up to see her. They didn't knock, the body-guard let them in – he'd been sitting on a stool outside the door.

171

"He jumped," she told them. "He just took up position like a high-jumper and then simply disappeared."

The police said that such things happen. You can never really do anything. People make up their minds and then nothing can stop them. They imagine the actual leap and then suddenly just enter the world of their imagination and close the door after them. It had even happened in the police service. They tried to comfort her, though it wasn't at all necessary. Before they went they asked for her autograph – they pulled off their jackets and she wrote on their backs with a thick marker pen. And she gave them a handful of free tickets that Uncle Erland had had with him. She had to be in the municipal park at eight o'clock.

"Now you must come," she said.

"Me?" I said. "That will only make things worse. If you have to have me around too."

With that she blew down the telephone at me, long and slow; it was as if she was trying to remind me of some secret that I'd perhaps forgotten.

"You've got your plastic surgeon," I said. "And your body-guard."

"That's not the same," Paula replied. "It's not at all as simple as you think."

As if I could still imagine that anything was simple.

"I'll come," I said. "I'll leave everything else. As soon as I've sorted things out and am free, I'll come."

She would be in Halmstad the next day. I arranged permanent forwarding of my mail to her address in Stockholm. All I took with me were the Madonna and the black wooden chest that now held a few coins and banknotes again. And two volumes of Schopenhauer.

She collected me from the station. She was staying at the Tylöhus Hotel. It was almost five o'clock.

Everyone knows what happened in Halmstad that evening.

She laughed when she saw the luggage I was carrying – I had tied a rope round the Madonna and was carrying her with my artificial hand. I didn't think Paula looked shaken or even upset; she said that it might rain before evening. She liked rain: the audience were always more serious and sensible if it rained on them a little. But she took hold of my left hand and squeezed it hard and only let go of it when the car arrived. The bodyguard was at the wheel.

We said nothing about Uncle Erland. We talked about the houses we passed and their gardens. I'd never been in Halmstad before. It might seem strange, but we never did get to talk to each other properly about Uncle Erland. We just mentioned him, because it was unavoidable, and most of what happened later was due to him. Neither Paula nor I had anything to say about him; we didn't even bother about his funeral. Someone took charge of him and made sure he got buried. The newspapers probably had long reports about him, but we didn't read any newspapers. We were busy with other things. And we wouldn't have been able to decide what kind of funeral he should have had anyway.

The bodyguard brought food, and we ate in Paula's room – pizza and kebabs – using the folded Madonna as a table. I told her that I'd redirected my mail to her address. "That's fine," she said. "We can help one another take care of everything." Then she asked whether I ever got any mail.

When I thought about it I had to admit that it was a long time since I'd had any letters. But people often used to write to me before, I said.

That was the only aspect of the future we talked about, the mail that I'd arranged to have forwarded and that I would probably never get. She ate two whole pizzas, and I told her about the barman in Texas who'd eaten twenty pizzas and drunk five litres of beer in an hour. His photo was in *The Guinness Book of Records*. We laughed together and breathed garlic fumes at one another. Paula showed me a home-made nightdress she'd received from an admirer in Vänersborg, with BLOOD AND FIRE across the chest, one of Paula's lyrics, that he'd embroidered on it himself. She seemed happy. I

173

thought to myself that she didn't really need me at all. But she'd convinced herself that she ought to need someone. And I happened to be the one.

Then she wanted me to go with her to the park. I tried to tell her that I would just feel in the way, that I didn't want to be trampled underfoot; I thought that what happened in the park should remain a matter between her and her audience, it was too private and delicate, I was an outsider and ought to keep away. But it was no use.

"You don't understand anything," she said. "I won't get through it on my own."

That's how it came about that I was there. And I forgot to ask what it was she couldn't get through on her own.

I sat in the dressing room with her while she put on her make-up and did her exercises and warmed up her voice. Out on the stage a group from Gothenburg was playing, entertaining the audience until it was time for Paula to appear. We could hear the drums and the bass guitar, but nothing else. Her own musicians were standing out in the corridor smoking and talking and laughing. Paula didn't need anyone to help her, it was obvious she'd done the whole thing hundreds of times before, and she looked as if she'd forgotten that I was sitting there. The roar and buzz of the crowd was audible too, but as if in the far distance. As she undressed and put on her costume for the first number she hummed "Sheep May Safely Graze".

I looked at her. She had a beautiful body. I'd never thought about it before.

Then someone gave three knocks on the door – it might have been the bodyguard – it was the signal that meant it was time for her to go on. The rabbit was tied up where it should be, the projector was set, the musicians were in their places, she was awaited. The group playing out on stage fell silent and the noise from the audience seemed a little more muffled and subdued. "I'm going to pretend that you're the audience," she said. "No one else." And she ran off and slammed the door so quickly that I had no time to react.

I didn't want to hear anything. I bent forward and put my hands over my ears. But my artificial hand didn't fit tightly, and so I heard what happened anyway.

She performed the movements the choreographer had worked out for her. Then she came to a stop up at the footlights. She was supposed to stand still and look pensive and sincere as she sang "Love and Peace and Understanding and Forgiveness and Tenderness".

I don't know how many times she raised her head and opened her mouth to begin singing, I only know that she didn't get out a single sound. The audience that had just established another astonishing record was completely silent; there wasn't a single movement or cough or clearing of throat, perhaps just a low, cautious groan as if they were trying to participate in Paula's effort. Again and again the musicians repeated the first chords, but she couldn't produce even a squeak or a whisper. It sounded as if she was blowing at the audience. Perhaps that was what she was doing.

In the end she gave up. She bent forward and hid her face in her hands as if she'd been overcome by some kind of shame, then rushed off the stage, tripped and fell twice over cables and leads and made her knees bleed, and dropped the white plastic dove she'd been holding in her hand.

It was to me she ran. She curled up on my lap and threw her arms round my neck exactly as she used to do when we were both little, although of course I must really have been almost grown up. We stayed sitting like that. And the audience was still silent.

But gradually we began to hear individual voices. They were shrill and powerful, you could imagine that people were trying to demonstrate the noise levels that could be reached with just a little effort. There was some whistling too. Then the screams got louder and more and more widespread. The musicians were trying to play but nobody was taking any notice of them. Finally the din grew so appalling that Paula and I wouldn't have been able to hear each other if we'd tried to say anything. The rain had started at last, but it didn't help. The musicians gave up and came rushing into the corridor. And the bodyguard opened the door and slipped in with us. He shouted something, but I don't know what.

"All hell's let loose," I think he was trying to say. "They'll kill us now."

Two policemen also arrived. They'd bolted all the doors and locked themselves in with us. "We're safe here," I read on the lips of one of them. How long we sat like that I don't know. Paula was completely immobile. I assume that initially she was paralysed with shock. She had never really understood how fervently the public loved her.

All this time the audience were hard at work outside. They were ripping up the floor of the stage board by board, and using the wood they'd torn loose to break all the windows and to smash against the walls in their attempts to get in. One of the policemen came over and held up a scrap of paper on which he'd written: "The army is on its way." I don't know whether that was true or not.

Luckily someone had got a can of petrol to set light to the building. That was our salvation.

The fire brigade arrived. The fire had already taken good hold, and one end of the building was engulfed in flames. The firemen brought in all the fire engines and hoses they had, and it had an effect – the audience fled, we heard the noise dying away, it sounded like a thunderstorm receding, and the water came pouring in on us through a hole the audience had managed to make in the roof.

We were driven back to the hotel in one of the fire engines. Paula's bodyguard was shaking and trembling so much that he could scarcely walk, and the firemen had to support him. He was saying over and over again: "God help me. God help me."

When we got to the hotel we had to undress him and put him to bed – his room was next to Paula's – and then we changed into dry clothes ourselves and sat in Paula's room. When the telephone rang I pulled out the plug. We had a bottle of vodka that Paula had probably got as a treat for me, and we used the tooth mug. I'd put the

Madonna and the wooden chest under Paula's bed, thinking that the bodyguard would be able to look after them all together. I pulled out the chest now and showed her the money. I said that it felt as if I'd somehow started again from the beginning, not my own beginning but my great-grandfather's. Paula thought it was really rather a lot of money. She has never properly understood what money is and has never been able to tell the difference between large sums and small.

Then I asked her whether she had simply lost her voice. It was the wrong question, because she was talking to me anyway. But I wanted to understand what had happened. Or: I pretended that I had to understand.

She didn't laugh at me, nor did she get angry, she just looked at me as if I'd said something significant, something that she would have to give some thought to. And a few moments later she started to sing, sitting leaning forward in the chair with her elbows on her knees, smiling a little as if we'd still been talking about the money in the chest or the home-made nightdress. She didn't look as if she was exerting herself at all, yet her voice must have been audible all over the hotel and out across the beach and sea below us. It was that Bach cantata. She took a little break between "He who abides by the truth" and "will rest at peace for ever in the hands of the Lord," and had a sip of vodka. When she'd finished we sat in silence for some time. I said that I hadn't managed the diphthongs, I wasn't a proper translator. And then Paula attempted to explain what had happened to her on the stage in the park.

When she had made her entrance the light from the spotlights was supposed to be waiting for her and she had to dance straight towards its source. The light would blind her, as it had night after night. But here in Halmstad the technicians had made a mistake, and the light was still on the musicians when she came out, and she wasn't blinded. For one or two seconds she was able to look round.

She saw the audience and herself and the monstrous portrait of her little mother and the darkness of evening and the rabbit. There was really nothing special in all that, but she'd never seen it before. And she simply couldn't manage to sing.

But that was hardly an explanation. I said as much: "That doesn't sound particularly credible."

"It doesn't matter," she replied. "Whatever happens, there's never any explanation that's adequate."

"You must try your best," I said, and took a good swig of the vodka. "If you can't make everything intelligible to me, I'll never be able to help you."

"Are you going to help me?"

"Who else?" I said. "There isn't anyone else."

"I was thinking of Uncle Erland," she continued. "And of you, sitting in my dressing room with your eyes closed and your hands over your ears."

"Yes. That's what I was doing."

"Something snapped inside me."

"I've heard that such things can occur," I said. "But I don't understand it."

"Something just went," said Paula. "I could almost hear it happening inside me."

"I can't understand how anything can break inside us," I said. "That's not how we're made."

"Don't you remember the clothes line we climbed along and broke? Something like that."

"No," I said. "I don't remember. And why were you thinking of Uncle Erland?"

Paula had some salami in one of her suitcases. We shared it. We stood by the window as we ate, and tried to see the sea.

Then she told me why she'd been thinking of Uncle Erland, and what she imagined had happened to him.

"I think it was I who did it," she said.

"Did what?"

"Killed Uncle Erland."

"He did it himself," I said. "He jumped out of the window. You were standing there and saw it happen, you said so yourself."

"I threw him," said Paula. "I think we were standing facing each other and I just did it, I changed my grip twice and then he was gone."

"You could never have managed it," I said. "You're too small and light. And you had no reason to do it."

"I had a self-defence teacher," Paula said. "Two days a week for six months. Uncle Erland arranged it."

"Of course," I said. "Self-defence. That's an entirely different matter."

We'd finished the salami. And the vodka bottle was almost empty.

"It's dangerous to think that way. We always have feelings of guilt. And a guilt complex can make us imagine anything."

"Why should I have feelings of guilt?"

"We imagine all kinds of things," I replied. "We bury ourselves in self-reproach. And in the end our imaginings turn themselves into real people and real events."

"I've never needed to imagine anything," Paula said. "Everything has always been enough in itself."

He had wanted to talk to her. At long last. And explain things. She didn't understand him, since he'd always talked to her as much as he wanted to. He had stood before her with tears in his eyes and said that she was the only person who really meant anything to him. From now on he would devote all his energies to her, he wouldn't concern himself with anybody else. Admittedly he was her creator, so to speak, but she had become immeasurably greater than he could ever have imagined when he created her. She had become like a daughter to him – more even than that: he wanted to be both a father and a mother to her. From now on their roles would be reversed, the power and authenticity of her artistry had conquered him, he would do whatever she asked of him, he would serve her humbly to the best of his ability.

"Dear Uncle Erland," she said, "if I hadn't had you I would be absolutely nothing, I wouldn't exist if you hadn't taken me in hand."

And she had looked deep into his eyes and stretched out her arms towards him.

"Can you show me what you imagine you did?" I asked, placing myself in front of her.

I don't remember exactly what happened next.

When I came to my senses I was lying on the floor with my head half inside the bedside table, my back aching and pains in my knees and feet. My artificial hand had come off and landed under the bed – I noticed it immediately, it had really come to feel part of me. Paula was still standing by her chair, holding one of my shoes and trying to read the brand name on the underside of the sole.

It took a few moments for me to struggle to my feet. She helped me fasten the artificial hand back on – I couldn't manage it myself. We sat down and shared the last drop of vodka between us.

"There, you see," I said. "You can't have done it. The way you throw, he wouldn't have fallen down to the street, he'd have finished up in the wall of the house opposite. And you can't aim, you would never have hit the window."

"No," she said. "That's what I thought."

"And you would never have been able to bring yourself to do it," I went on. "You can't manage without him."

"That's true," said Paula.

"And you wouldn't have just stood there calmly reading 'Aristocrat' on the sole."

"No, I suppose I wouldn't."

"We must never let our imagination get the better of us," I continued. "We must always make sure we're master of it. If we let our imagination take command, then the false and the genuine merge into one and we become completely helpless."

"Yes," said Paula.

"You ought to take off your make-up," I said.

She still had her stage face on; neither of us had thought of it. She looked as if she was made of porcelain. Or plastic. It took her at least a quarter of an hour to wash and rub herself clean. When she came back from the bathroom she smelled of solvent. But she was herself again. That was the last time she took off a mask. I think she knew that.

I can't remember us sleeping that night. We sat and dozed and talked and just let the time go past. When it began to get light I rang and ordered a car to take us to Stockholm. And I phoned Paula's doctor, the plastic surgeon. She needed a certificate, I said, she would have to cancel the six remaining performances. No, there was nothing to worry about, she was just tired and overworked and hoarse, terribly hoarse. Yes, I would pass on the message that he was missing her. And he promised to make copies of the certificate and post them to the organisers – I gave him the addresses. I wrote short notes to the musicians that Paula signed and the receptionist dealt with: the tour was over, it had been a wonderful time and she loved them; Paula Music Ltd would pay their wages according to contract. Love and kisses. I left Paula's make-up box in reception and told them to burn it. I also phoned the Central News Agency: Paula had gone down with a simple throat infection and needed a short period of rest; she'd soon be back again.

Before we left we looked in on the bodyguard. He was lying awake on his bed staring up at the ceiling, and still trembling. We asked whether he wanted to come with us, there was room in the car for him too. But he just shook his head: he didn't dare, he would try to smuggle himself on to a train later in the day. Paula bent over him and kissed him on the forehead and both cheeks. I didn't understand that. I didn't realise how close they'd been. Or however you describe it.

It was half past five in the morning, and we didn't think anyone would see us or be interested in us. We stood in the foyer with our luggage while we waited for the car.

But a young girl came over to us; she'd been sitting curled up behind a pillar, waiting – she might have been about sixteen, no more. Her face was scratched and bloody, one eye was obscured by a red swelling and her clothes were hanging on her in tatters. She was carrying a little bundle in her arms.

"You're fantastic," she said to Paula. "You're greater than anything else I've ever experienced."

"Thank you," Paula replied.

She undid her bundle. There sat the rabbit.

She told us how she'd saved it. She'd been standing nearest the stage, and when the uproar had started she'd climbed up on someone's shoulders and chewed and bitten off the rabbit's string. She'd hidden the animal in her clothes and fought and crawled and pushed her way to the exit, getting knocked down again and again and nearly being trampled underfoot. But she'd managed it, she seemed to remember it taking her several hours, she'd really risked her life. But the rabbit had lived. God be praised.

She handed the rabbit to Paula. The girl's hands were torn and bloody too. She couldn't help laughing in her adoration and her pride.

Then she ran off.

That reminded us of the other rabbits. They were in a cage somewhere in the cellar. I told the receptionist that the kitchen could have them.

Just as the car drew up outside the glass doors a photographer arrived, God knows where from. Photographers turn up at any time and any place. We didn't have a chance to escape him – he took the last photo of Paula: no, not just of Paula, of us. The folded Madonna is leaning against my knee, the floor around us is covered in Paula's suitcases, we look tired and indifferent. In front of us, on my case, is the black wooden chest. And the rabbit is nestling as snug as can be in my artificial hand.

The car was comfortable, and we fell asleep almost immediately and slept all the way to Stockholm. We woke up just the once, in the village of Ödeshög, where we stopped and had a pizza. Opposite the pizzeria was a flock of sheep in a field. I carried the rabbit over there and set it down. It was Paula's suggestion. It's grazing there on mayweed and poppies to this day. I rang Paula Music Ltd in Stockholm from Ödeshög. I spoke to a secretary. She probably didn't know who I was, but I didn't need to explain, she knew everything already. She was crying and wailing so continuously and so wretchedly that I had to tell her that all this was only temporary and transient, Paula wasn't finished, none of it would last. Everything must be cancelled, recording sessions and concerts and interviews and rehearsals and advertising arrangements and lunches and travel schedules. There's no difference between "for good" and "for the moment". Everything has to draw to a close sooner or later.

"Stand by," I said.

"Yes," she sniffed, "we'll stand by."

THIS ACCOUNT is nearing its end. It really does have an end. Nothing more can happen after that. It's a happy ending; no one has ever achieved a happier ending to a story. Yet I'm sorry, because my left hand has improved considerably and is writing now with great facility.

We shut ourselves in Paula's apartment. We no longer had a bodyguard, the telephone plug was pulled out, the newspapers that came were thrown straight into the rubbish chute unread, and we didn't bother with the TV or radio. We played noughts and crosses. And poker patience. We listened to Mahler and Bruckner and Brahms and Prokofiev. Occasionally Paula would sit at the piano and play. Satie and Debussy and Schumann. We had our food brought up to us from Nico's Pizzeria down on the corner. Nico bought beer and aquavit for us too. I gave him the parrot that Paula had got from Uncle Erland, and he was pleased. Parrots can reach almost any age, and he's probably still there in Nico's Pizzeria imitating Paula. The oldest parrot in the world is 104 years old, living in Libourne in France. I've forgotten who owns it. We read the books I had with me. And Paula read poetry to me. She had once answered an advertisement in *Svenska Dagbladet* and bought two thousand volumes of poetry that a schoolteacher in Stockholm had left when he died. Entirely nature poetry. If I'd had my mandolin, I'd have tried to play *"O Sole Mio"* for her. We each spent half an hour a day jumping on the trampoline in Paula's bedroom. We cycled on her exercise bike. There was a video attached to the handlebars, showing the road and the countryside we were cycling through. As far as I remember we wanted for nothing.

The plastic surgeon came three times a week. She didn't go to his consulting rooms any more, he came to her. I would withdraw and leave them in peace. They would sit in the living-room for a while, and then shut themselves in her bedroom. But the walls were thin, and if I didn't turn on the stereo I could hear everything they did. He was an energetic and noisy lover, perhaps somewhat over-anxious.

He was very regular in his habits. Paula told me why that was.

He belonged to a small congregation with a church in Östermalm in central Stockholm. He could allow himself some time with her after the services without anyone missing him. That was the only free time he had, otherwise he was always expected to be in two places at once, at his consulting rooms in Stockholm and at his clinic in the country manor-house.

On one occasion when Paula was still in the bathroom I took him to one side and asked him whether he couldn't possibly find opportunities to come more often.

"Paula is restless and uneasy," I said. "As if she'd lost something. She sometimes wanders around in here not knowing what to do with herself; she slams doors and calls out to people who don't exist. As if it isn't enough for her to have been set free from that career."

But it was completely impossible for him. When he'd been smitten by Paula his life had been on the verge of breaking apart. But even so he had managed to create a structure that had also left space for her.

"A kind of equilibrium," he said. "But if just half an hour were to be altered, I'd be finished."

A letter arrived from the bank back home. My loan was due for repayment, and I hadn't paid the instalments and interest as I should have done. I'd forgotten that loan; I took it out to be able to insure the Madonna, in what seemed the long-distant past. "I herewith assign my house to the bank," I wrote in my reply. "Sell the house to release me from my debts, I'm never coming back, and I herewith also transfer ownership of the contents to the bank." I did my best with that letter, I wanted to be formal and correct. "If a surplus should remain from the sale," I wrote, "it is my wish that such amount should be used to erect a memorial stone to Paula's mother in the churchyard." I gave details of the house by name and number, and my own personal identification number and Paula's mother's name, and Paula and the plastic surgeon witnessed my signature and confirmed that I was in full possession of my faculties.

I had set up the Madonna in Paula's living-room. We'd got used to her and she'd almost become part of the furniture.

After having presented my property to the bank I lay awake all night. I was uneasy, yet I regretted nothing and wanted for nothing. I had become humbler and poorer, as if the house had been a personal attribute of myself, a character trait or an ability that I'd lost. I had always imagined myself in that house.

When the morning papers came I got up and took them out to the rubbish chute. Then I sat down on the floor in front of the Madonna. And something happened that was now inevitable whenever I gave myself the time to look at her properly: she turned dark and dull in some way, as if the clear enamel surface had softened and disintegrated, she lost her glow. And the red dot, Goatee's discreet signature, became enlarged and extended until I could soon see nothing else. That didn't mean she turned into a forgery for me: I realised it was just something I was imagining. But she changed, as if she herself had taken off a mask that had covered her before. She didn't become more genuine or more false, neither the one nor the other, but a third concept, something which no longer concerned me: what I saw were three more or less arbitrarily joined sections full of shapes and colours. And I thought to myself that I must have patience, eventually I'll begin to understand her again, I haven't lost her for good, I'll just have to learn to see her like this too.

After a while Paula came and sat down on the floor a few yards away from me, also to look at the Madonna. She had her little cassette player on her lap, and I could just faintly hear that she was listening to herself, a recording of "Oh Mother's Milk and Tears, Liquors and Potions of My Life" that she'd made only a few weeks before. I raised my right arm up in front of my chest and practised gripping movements in the air with my artificial hand. She was miming to the music, her lips and throat moving as if she were singing at the top of her voice.

I sat thinking of everything I'd lost. My house and furniture and art books, the picture-framing business, my right hand, my mandolin, Paula's mother, the oil paintings, the money in the chest, my grandfather, the first Madonna, the view from the kitchen window, Grandfather's piano and the whole of my way of life. I rubbed my bald pate with my left hand.

I know now what Paula was thinking about too: her little mother, her childhood, Uncle Erland, her brilliant career, her glove puppets, her public's love for her, her musicians, her father, *This Week*, her bodyguard, her make-up case, her music and the meaning of life. Everything she had lost.

Suddenly she started screaming at me. "I have no life outside this tiny apartment," she howled. "You've taken everything away from me." She wasn't looking at me, she was just shrieking as shrilly and scornfully as her strength allowed and counting up everything that had gone forever and that I had robbed her of. I of all people. It was ghastly. I couldn't help answering her charges. I set to with such force that I had a feeling that my larynx would burst. Of course I was guilty, I'd never in all my years said anything other than that I was guilty. But it was also her fault that I had lost absolutely everything – if it hadn't been for her my life would have been ridiculously simple, I would have stuck to my little craft and my oil paintings and my mandolin. But my life had got too big for me now: it was the Madonna's fault, but above all her, Paula's, fault. I wished that she'd never been born or that she'd had the sense to get herself killed in one of the mishaps that seemed to swarm around her like flies whatever she did. Uncle Erland might have been good enough to take her with him when he jumped out of the window. We screamed at the tops of our voices to shout each other down and not to have to hear any of it. She would have liked to claw my eyes out but she couldn't for the life of her bring herself to do that, she didn't even want to touch me with her little fingernail, I was so abominable. How long we went on like that I don't know, but in the end we were utterly empty and exhausted and just crumpled up and fell into total silence.

Now on top of everything else we had lost one another. And thus in a way ourselves.

I realised that it wasn't something that happened precisely there and then; it was a gradual fading and exploitation that had been going on all our lives or at least through the whole of this account; Paula and I had merely been the objects or instruments that an unwritten story had needed and used for its own forward movement, a story that funnily enough claimed to be the story of us. The two selves that we had till then called our own, my self and Paula's, were both involuntary actors or objects that events had appropriated in order to take place. Simply existing was not enough.

So we sat there, I in my pyjamas and she in her crocheted night-dress, staring down at the floor and not being able to do anything. The clock that she'd got from Uncle Erland chimed every half hour from the top of the television set. Paula sighed occasionally; I didn't even do that.

We must have been sitting brooding like that for two or three hours when Paula said: "How should we really live our lives?"

"Yes," I said, "how the hell should we? If only we knew."

At that moment the mail arrived. We could hear the postman pouring letters through the letter-box. I stood up and stretched my arms and legs and went out to the hall to pick it all up. There were about fifty letters for Paula, and I put them in a plastic bag and carried them over to the rubbish chute. There was one for me. Forwarded. It was my second letter since I'd left home.

I had a shower before I opened it; I wanted to be clean when I read it. I took my time, and if I remember rightly I also treated myself to a yoghurt. Then I sat down on the sofa with my letter.

I was now conclusively cleared of all suspicion, the tax authorities back home wrote. Or more precisely, the tax inspector I knew so well, the girl who'd once written a thesis entitled *Dreams Beneath an Arctic Sky*. All confiscated property would be returned to my home. After certain formalities had been completed I could collect the *Madonna with the Dagger* from the local magistrate's office myself. Nils de Dardel's painting. The authorities had found that my affairs were in an almost unimaginable disorder and that there was a complete lack of book-keeping, but it was nevertheless quite clear that I had not cheated society in any way. They would recommend that I consider handing over the running of my financial affairs to a professional, which would give me greater opportunity to devote myself to purely creative activity. On a little piece of yellow paper clipped to the back of the letter the tax inspector had written: "How wonderful that you've finally been awarded a clean bill of health! You ought to be given a guardian! Lots of love!"

As Paula and I sat reading the letter, and Paula said calmly and rather coolly "You'll be leaving me now", the doorbell rang.

I opened the door. It was a bald-headed man in a dark suit, carrying a bulky briefcase under his arm. He introduced himself and asked if he could come in.

He wanted to be left alone with Paula.

"I'm afraid that's not possible," I said. "I'm the one who's taking care of everything for her."

Paula nodded, that was right.

"Including her financial affairs?" he asked.

Perhaps he recognised me. He was probably interested in art. And read the evening papers.

"Yes," I replied. "From now on all responsibilities are mine."

Paula confirmed that too. She even said it aloud: "His name is Theodore Marklund. I have no one else. He has taken over everything."

He was a lawyer. Crackshot, Uncle Erland, had been his client. He shook my artificial hand and held it for a long time as he looked deep into my eyes.

Perhaps he should have come earlier, he went on. But it had been hard to get hold of Paula, she didn't answer letters and the telephone wasn't working.

"We've pulled out the plug," I explained.

He also had to be very careful, a lawyer must never be too hasty or precipitate. But now all the formalities had been completed and Paula could receive her inheritance.

"What inheritance?" I asked.

The legacy of Mr Noldeby, Crackshot, Uncle Erland.

"No," said Paula. "No."

Yes, he had left everything to her in his will. It was the most moving will the lawyer had ever seen. Did we want him to read it to us? It was really on a much higher plane and more spiritual than a normal earthly will, it was a declaration of love, it was the Song of Songs in a modern idiom.

"No, thank you," I said. "We'll take your word for it."

He had to sit down while he listed everything that Paula had inherited. He read from a bundle of papers he had taken out of the briefcase.

Property. Stocks and shares. Money. Singers. Two ice-hockey players and a footballer. Works of art. A spiritual medium. Options and promissory notes. Diamonds. A motor yacht in the archipelago. Gold ingots. Two cars. A nightclub in Heidenheim in Germany. I can't remember everything.

And Paula Music Ltd. She had inherited herself. Even more, in fact: all the rights to herself.

"Those sportsmen and artistes," I said. "You must let them go."

"Good Lord," the lawyer said, "who'll look after them then?"

Paula spoke up. "Leave them to someone else," she said. "We don't want them. We would ruin their lives. Completely."

It was beautiful to hear her use that little word again. "We."

"The spiritual medium," I said. "What's that used for?"

"She speaks with the dead," the lawyer answered. "Paula gets twenty per cent on every seance. Very popular."

"Sell her," I said. "We won't deal in humbug and deception."

As we were talking he was making little notes on his papers.

"With all the dead?" Paula asked. "With any dead person?"

"I assume so," said the lawyer. "I haven't heard of any exceptions."

Paula and I were still in our nightclothes; we were bewildered and confused. Yet we were speaking more clearly and lucidly than ever before. I was rubbing my bald pate so hard that I got blood on my fingertips.

"Paula wants cash," I said. "Nothing but cash."

I didn't even bother to ask about the works of art. It could be a whole museum for all I cared, I didn't want to know about them.

"That's right," said Paula. "Just cash."

But the lawyer didn't want to go along with that at all. He was smiling at us, in a friendly or perhaps indulgent manner, but as he spoke he kept beating his knuckles on the briefcase as if to emphasise how serious he really was. What Paula had in her hands was neither more nor less than the germ of a handy little financial empire. A management company with an appropriate number of subsidiaries would undoubtedly be the most fitting and promising solution. The total assets could if necessary be transferred to Paula Music Ltd. He ventured to predict that Paula would soon be quoted on the stock exchange. In the course of time her name would have the same resonance as Custos or Providentia or Nobel.

Paula said nothing. But her cheeks were quivering and I could see she would soon start crying.

"I've been involved in business all my life," I said. "I know what's best for Paula."

"Throwing away the work of a lifetime," the lawyer said. "I'm truly glad that Mr Noldeby isn't here to see what's going on. Crackshot."

"We are mourning Uncle Erland too," I said. "We shall do our utmost to honour his memory."

He then tried to persuade us at least to wait for a while, not just to rush blindly ahead in our sorrow and despair.

But I was obdurate. I drummed on the desk with my artificial hand. One week, and then that little germ of a financial empire should be dismantled.

He relented when I promised him eight per cent of all profits and all monies obtained from the sales.

He drew up a power of attorney for himself, writing it on the back of an advertisement for the spiritual medium, and Paula signed it.

Before he went he asked about the Madonna. He'd recognised her. He pointed at her and said he would be pleased to offer his services in disposing of her too. While he was about it.

"No," I said, "I'll take care of her myself. She belongs to one of my own enterprises."

When we were alone again Paula climbed up on to my lap. I felt as if she was only two or three years old again and needed to have her hair stroked and be kissed on the cheek and patted on the back. She was trembling, and hid her face in her hands. "Everything will be fine now," I said, "soon there'll be no more problems in the whole world, any day now we'll be as free and happy as two canaries."

In the end she calmed down again. She raised her head and dried her eyes with the back of her hands and asked: "How did you know that he should have precisely eight per cent?"

"There are unwritten rules," I said, "in the business world. You needn't worry about it."

After a while she got up and went over to the piano and played "The Bees' Wedding" for me. She knew it by heart. And I quickly put in the telephone plug and rang down to Nico's to order two pizzas. The ones called De Luxe. With fillet of beef and Béarnaise sauce.

We stayed there in the living-room the whole of that day, I in my pyjamas and Paula in her crocheted nightdress with BLOOD AND FIRE across the chest. We started gradually talking about the future. We drank beer and aquavit with the pizzas. But we didn't use the word 'future'; we tried to pretend it was something else we were talking about. In fact it probably was; what we were glimpsing was something much bigger and more enduring than the future. Paula wanted to be alone with the telephone for a few minutes, so I went and sat in the bathroom. "A little business secret," she said, blushing slightly and waving her fingers in the air ambiguously. She's going to phone him, I thought to myself.

As we'd sat talking I'd been laying out my patience cards. And at six o'clock that evening it came out. It was the first time in my life, I'd never thought it could happen with the Demon.

As I sat staring at the cards that had arranged themselves so unexpectedly and wondrously, there was a ring at the door. The lawyer must have forgotten something, I thought to myself, and has come back. But it was Nico.

He'd brought Paula's secret. It wasn't what I'd imagined at all. It was Nico she'd telephoned; she'd asked him to go down to the Salvation Army music shop on Östermalmsgatan. He was holding a mandolin. For me. It had a decorated border and a curved base.

For the rest of the evening I reclined on the sofa doing my very best to start teaching my artificial hand *"O Sole Mio"*.

I'VE ASKED Paula, but she remembers nothing of what we did for the rest of that week. At first I couldn't understand how that could be, because generally she remembers almost everything. I've since realised that it's completely natural, that those seven days have been transformed into a distant echo of the present, everything we thought out and dreamed about has become solid reality – the fulfilment is so strong that it has erased the original conception. Painters often draw on the canvas with charcoal or chalk, then the drawing is covered in paint, and all traces of it disappear.

We were planning our future, down to the smallest detail.

The lawyer came at five o'clock every afternoon. Paula lit candles and put on the stereo, playing Verdi's *Requiem*, "Lux aeterna" and "Libera me". He would be carrying two thick briefcases, and twice he also brought flowers for Paula. We moved the table aside and made him empty the briefcases on the floor in front of the sofa.

On the first evening he didn't want to do this, but I said that naturally we had to count it. In my family we'd always counted money lying on the floor, it was restful for the back and nothing can fall down or fly away and disappear.

Paula had to sign the receipts.

Of course we never did count it; amounts of that size don't need to be counted. And how do you add dollars to yen, and marks to Swiss francs? Money in absolutely pure form is also slightly repellent, representing nothing but itself, or anything at all, it's a kind of phantom. We just arranged it in bundles and packed it into the black wooden chest. Paula had to get into the chest from time to time and tread it down.

It was Friday afternoon when the lawyer presented his final account. Paula signed her name on a hundred or so documents. And I had to sign three or four, but the lawyer probably just wanted to please me, since it could hardly have been necessary. There still remained a few small affairs to finalise, and he would be back in due course; we would have more than enough to do for several years investing the considerable sums he'd already brought us.

"Yes, indeed," we said. "We have all the time in the world now."

We knew that we would never see him again.

On the Saturday morning I set off on my journey, and I was back again Sunday evening. I travelled by car and plane. I had phoned and arranged the times and places for my visits, and I was expected everywhere I went. In some places even welcomed. The newspapers doubtless wrote various things about that expedition afterwards, I don't know. I shall give an account here only of the salient points, mainly the route, and nothing else.

I went first to Dieter Goldmann in Karlstad. I had wrapped the Madonna in corrugated cardboard and carried her by a string. He didn't look the way I'd imagined, he was small and slight and white-haired and had big sorrowful eyes. He didn't proffer his hand but just patted my arm carefully and sensitively.

"I've realised that she isn't mine," I said. "She belongs to the Goldmann family."

"Yes, yes," Dieter Goldmann said. "In a double sense. Will you come with me to see her grave?"

He was speaking of his mother, the woman who had modelled for the Madonna.

"Thank you," I said, "but unfortunately I haven't time. I would have been pleased to; but I can't fit it in."

"You must have had expenses," he said.

"Yes," I replied. And named the amount.

He made no difficulties, he didn't even try to argue, he was prepared. He disappeared for a few moments, then came back with the

195

money in a bicycle saddlebag made of black plastic. "Won't you count it?" he asked.

"I've never cheated anyone," I said. "Why should anyone cheat me?"

Then he seemed to forget me. He opened her up straight away and put her against two trestles that he'd set up in the living-room. He got down on his knees and stuck his head under her to look for the W.G. that was carved into the panel at the back.

"Inheritance," I said, "weighs more heavily than anything else. Our lives are bound up in our inheritance like pupae in their chrysalids."

"Yes," he said. "Or vice versa."

Then he was silent. Presumably he was just so happy that he couldn't speak.

"There's a small spot of crimson appeared here," I said, pointing to the tiny dot of red paint. "I think it can be picked off. With a sharp knife."

But he didn't hear me.

Maria was at home alone, the woman who'd lived with me almost a whole autumn. She looked exactly as I remembered her, possibly just a little fatter. "He's hardly ever at home," she said. "I don't see much of him at all at weekends."

"Are you happy?" I asked. "Do you love him?"

"Sometimes. Though really I've never loved anyone but you."

"I've known that all along," I said. "It's good to hear you say it."

"In actual fact I don't understand how we could ever have given one another up," she went on. "Now that I see you."

She was really looking at me.

"It was pure chance," I said. "We might equally well have stayed together all our lives."

Then I showed her the letter from the tax authorities.

"She belongs to both of us. But I want you to have her. She fits much better into your life than mine."

196

"You're altogether too honourable," she said. "And honest. You're quite simply too good for this world."

"You shouldn't say that," I replied. "I just act as well as I can."

I got her to read the agreement I'd written. She bought me out of the Madonna, she paid such and such an amount for my share, and she would be able to collect her from the magistrate's office a week later, when all the formalities were completed.

She pulled out two bundles of banknotes from her handbag.

"Will this be enough?"

"Yes," I said, weighing them in my artificial hand. "That's more than enough."

I stuffed the money into the cycle bag I'd brought with me from Karlstad.

Before I left she wanted to kiss me one last time. I remembered the taste. Some sort of chewing gum. Or mothballs.

The bank manager back home was touched. "Having such trust in me," he said. He wanted to invite me to dinner. But I didn't have the time. Or at least a glass of brandy. "I drink nothing but pure aquavit," I said.

And he actually had a decanter of unspiced German schnaps, Nordischer Löwe.

My little debt would soon be settled, he explained. The house was already sold, and the bank had had the contents taken to a flea-market. And there was a surplus. Of course it was a shame that I was leaving in this way, I would be missed by all my friends and neighbours, in fact most of them had already begun to miss me several weeks before. "But you're too big for this little town," he said, "with all your ideas, and your philosophy of life."

He got me to sign a few papers concerning the house. And he showed me a sketch of the memorial stone to Paula's mother. The bank had commissioned it from a local artist. Black granite, half a hand sticking up from the top as if someone was being crushed inside the stone, and a dove hovering beneath the hand. EVER

TOWARDS YOU THE MISTS OF MY STORMY SOUL SHALL RISE, the words ran. And her name and dates.

"That's fine," I said. "Perfect. Baudelaire. Paula will be pleased."

Then the bank manager bought the Madonna from me. In cash. He would be able to collect her himself in a week's time from the magistrate's office. I put the money in the black plastic cycle bag.

Gulliver offered me a meal of bread and thick slices of sausage. He didn't have any aquavit; we drank Coca-Cola.

"I can't go on any longer," I said. "I'm giving up now."

"That's good," he said. "To hear that you've finally come to your senses."

"I thought I could cope with it," I said. "But I've had sleepless nights for weeks. I don't think I can manage to collect her from the magistrate's office."

"You've lost your nerve," he said.

"Yes. I've lost my nerve."

"You weren't tough enough," he said. "Sentimentality is your downfall. In business you have to be as hard as nails."

I even managed to make tears come to my eyes as I looked at him. His face was so loose and flabby that he could barely find his mouth to stuff the sausage in.

"God knows I've done my best," I said. "I thought life would be absolutely meaningless if I couldn't keep her."

"You're too small for this painting," he said. "I could see that straight away. If you'd understood that from the very beginning, you'd have avoided all this. It's a question of knowing your limitations."

"I thought that was the only reason I existed," I said. "To find the Madonna."

"We can never really know for sure," said Gulliver. "I believe God has a purpose with every single one of us. We live for a short time here in this vale of tears to be purified and cleansed."

I tapped miserably on the desk with the fingertips of my artificial hand. "This is dreadfully difficult for me," I said.

"You mustn't think that I'm not suffering with you," he said. "But for me it's purely a matter of principle. No one gets away with cheating me."

"I should have realised that," I said. "But I didn't know any better."

"I believe that's why we're here," said Gulliver. "To learn things. For eternity."

When I tried to give him a receipt for the money, he said: "We don't need any papers. Not between you and me. If you and I can't trust one another, then there's not much left to believe in. Then there would be no truth or justice in the world at all."

"No," I said. "That's true."

It was already evening when I got to the tax inspector's house. She was standing at the window waiting for me. She had put up her hair and tied it with a gold-coloured silk ribbon and put on powder and make-up so that I hardly recognised her. She was wearing a crimson dress with lace trimming over the breast.

"Are you going out somewhere?" I asked. "Have I come at a bad time?"

"I knew that you were coming," she replied. "I've been waiting for you."

"Good Lord," I said, "you shouldn't go to so much trouble for my sake."

She'd set out a meal for us on the dining table in the living-room. Crab.

"How did you know," I asked, "that crab is my favourite food?"

"You talk in your sleep," she replied. "Almost entirely about crab."

No one had told me before that I talk in my sleep. It felt as if she was suddenly very close to me.

"That was a fine dedication you wrote," I said. "In *Dreams Beneath an Arctic Sky*. That the content of a person's consciousness can be lifted out of him and become reality."

"Thank you," she said. And then she asked: "What have you got in that cycle bag?"

"Toothbrush," I said. "And pyjamas. I'm going to stay at a hotel."

"You can sleep here."

"No," I said. "I don't want to be any trouble. And I'm in a hurry."

"I thought it was really good that time," she said.

"It certainly was," I said. "It's a memory we should treasure."

I've always eaten more quickly than other people. And now I discovered that my artificial hand was perfect for eating crab with. There was no need for a fork.

"I've been thinking a lot about art and life lately," I said as I ate. "They're really two different worlds. If only we could think of a way of uniting them."

"Yes," she said. "That would be an art in itself."

"I've never really valued life as highly as it deserves," I went on. "And I've overestimated art."

"It's easily done," she said. "I've had periods like that too."

"You've been a great help to me," I said. "I've come to understand a lot of things because of you."

"I just do what I can," she said. "We can't do more than that."

She didn't eat the roe or liver, she just picked out what little meat she could find with her fork.

"I'll eat anything you leave," I said.

"Fine," she said. "I'm a rather fussy eater."

"Actually," I said, "I think you belong in the world of art. When you wrote *Dreams Beneath an Arctic Sky*, you were yourself. And I so very much want to help you."

"I'm not so sure that the difference is really very great," she said. "The only thing that matters is affection. In both art and life."

"I must free myself from art," I said. "And you must make your way back to it. That's why you must have the Madonna."

"But serving society can be quite fascinating too," she said.

"No one else would be able to buy her so cheaply," I said. "But to you I could practically give her away."

200

She handed me the crab shell, and it still had nearly everything left in it.

"I would never be able to find any joy in her," she said, "if I didn't know that I'd done the right thing."

"You've already given me so much," I said. "And now almost two whole crabs."

She went out into the kitchen, and I heard her washing her hands. There was even more roe in her crab than in mine. When she came back she was carrying an old blue mitten with embroidered stars on. The money was inside it.

"This is all I've been able to scrape together," she said. "We're not all that well paid. At the tax office."

I felt in the mitten with my left hand. There really wasn't very much.

"That's a fortune," I said. "And art prices have collapsed terribly. The market's more or less dead."

"You can never look at art like that," she said. "Art is a spiritual matter – it has nothing to do with money and markets."

"You can collect her in a week's time," I said.

"Yes," she replied, "I know the procedures."

Then I signed a purchase agreement and a receipt that she had written out. And stuffed the mitten in the cycle bag.

"You may not believe me," I said, "but this is a great relief for me. To be free of her. And to know that she's safe."

She stood at the window waving as I left. No, she wasn't waving, she was making clear vigorous signs with both hands. I recognised the message immediately. They were gestures Dardel used to make to his friends when they took their leave on a train or at an airport, meaning WE PROBABLY WON'T SEE ONE ANOTHER AGAIN AND WE DON'T GIVE A DAMN.

I stayed the night at a little guesthouse in one of the industrial settlements on the edge of the plain. The landlady recognised me. "New business in hand?" she said, and winked at me. I'd forgotten that anybody might recognise me. At first I thought of saying that she was mistaken, that I was someone else. But instead I just muttered something about irons in the fire and balls in the air and burning the candle at both ends and eggs in different baskets.

I rang Paula. "I soon won't need to worry any more," I said, "I'll soon be sure that someone will be looking after the Madonna." Then I fell asleep with the cycle bag as a pillow. It was nicely filled and firm.

The local magistrate said that he was flattered. He'd been expecting me to come and collect her, and when I'd phoned a few days before he'd been astonished and excited, yet at the same time he felt calm and confident. The Madonna belonged to him. In his heart he'd known it all along. The moment she was put in his care he'd realised that he could never bear to be parted from her. She'd been hung up not only on the wall of his office but also inside himself, so to speak. Humble adoration, that's how he would describe his feelings. "We art collectors," he said, "are like that. We live with our hearts in our mouths all the time."

"Yes," I said. "I know."

"What we collect," he continued, "is not artefacts or paintings, but circumstances and connections. Or correspondences. Between the collector-subject and the work-object. Permanent sensual stimulation, you could even say. Love that never dies." Would I perhaps like to see his collection?

"Thank you, but no. Time doesn't permit. And I've left all that behind me. I don't want to arouse my old self again."

We were sitting in a little lounge in his house. The walls were full of paintings, but I wasn't interested in them, I didn't want to see them. I hadn't been able to imagine in advance how painful it would be to sell the Madonna; it hurt just as much every time.

He wanted to discuss the price.

"No," I said. "That would degrade her."

"But it's an integral part, so to speak," he said. "It enhances the experience."

"No," I repeated.

"She'll be the most expensive work of art in my whole life."

"A real collector must have such an item," I replied.

"Really and truly she's too expensive for me," he said. "I ought to resist her. I'm going to regret it. The only sensible thing would be to forget her."

"I see."

But then he brought out the money; he'd been sitting on it: I'd thought it was a cushion. I gave him a receipt.

"It feels wonderful," he said. "I was afraid we wouldn't complete the deal. When you buy art you have to tread as carefully as on overnight ice. It can all crack without warning. An art deal is the most fragile and brittle bond that can unite two people."

When I opened the cushion and poured out the money into the cycle bag he said: "It's funny, I think counting money is detestable, too."

"It's the artificial hand," I said. "It's so damned insensitive. You simply can't count money with it."

By four o'clock I was back in Stockholm.

Goatee opened the door straight away when I rang. Exactly like last time, he'd been standing by the door waiting for me.

He was wearing a blue dressing gown with a monogram on the breast pocket. "I'm actually ill in bed," he said. "You must excuse me."

He went ahead of me to the Kandinsky room. He was a lamentable sight. His body had almost wasted away, his dressing gown was hanging limp and baggy on him, his skin was wrinkled and furrowed and yellow. His hands shook as he mixed me a *Für Immer Selig*.

"I'm not allowed to have it now," he said, handing me the glass. "But you have your life before you."

203

"How can you not be allowed to have anything?" I asked.

"As you can probably see, I'm dying," he said.

"Good Lord," I said. "Nobody would believe it. You've just lost a bit of weight, you look in good form."

"The doctors give me a month at most," he said. "Or it might happen even sooner."

"Why should you believe the doctors?" I said. "They're only human beings like us."

He'd sat down in the other armchair and folded his hands over his chest. I took a sip from my glass.

"But if things should go as badly as that, at least you've got an incredible life's work behind you."

"Yes," he said. "I often think that. It's a brilliant achievement. But also a problem. The moment I let the world know that it's my life's work it will cease to be incredible."

"Yes," I said. "That's obviously a slight snag."

"Questions about authentic and fake will follow us into death," he said.

"If we don't somehow manage to escape," I said. "And put both authenticity and falsehood behind us."

He smiled at that. "I've taught you something, anyway."

"That's what I imagine, at least," I said. "I don't know where the idea came from."

We sat for a while in silence. I drank.

"So you want to sell the Madonna," he said.

"Yes. The first Madonna. The original."

"In normal circumstances I would never even have considered buying her," he said. "But everything's different now."

"In the face of death," I said.

"Yes," he said. "In the face of death."

"I won't try to push you," I said. "You must do what you think is right. I would never be able to cheat anyone."

"Nothing has really changed," he said. "The first Madonna isn't any more authentic than the second."

"No," I said. "Both of them are genuine."

"But as the end draws near you get a bit sentimental," he said. "You become more open to the trivial and the conventional."

"I can imagine that," I said. "If there were any falseness, it would be destroyed by death."

"If I were to buy her now, it wouldn't be because my basic values had changed. I just feel a vague need to cover myself."

"Of course," I said. "Of course."

"Have you read Pascal?" he asked.

"Yes. I've read Pascal."

"When you look into eternity you somehow become insecure," he said. "All your convictions suddenly seem inadequate."

When I'd emptied my glass I said: "I've forgotten the recipe. I'd like to have it. As a keepsake." He fetched a pen and paper and wrote it down for me. *Für Immer Selig.*

"She would also be a curiosity in your collection," I said. "The Madonna."

"Yes," he said. "I'd thought of that too. A nice little irony. A joke. No one would understand it at all."

When we'd concluded our business he was so exhausted that he couldn't get up. I'd stuffed the money down into the cycle bag, he'd folded up the receipt and tucked it in the pocket with the monogram on. I lifted him up and carried him to his bed. Then I fetched my glass and bathed his forehead with the remaining drops in it. He opened his eyes and looked at me and said: "And I'd thought I was completely alone in the world."

"No," I said, "all solitude is just imagination. There is no true and genuine solitude."

Then he fell asleep. I locked the door behind me with his own key as I left, and put it back through the letter-box.

When I got home to Paula she took out two pizzas that she'd been keeping warm in the oven. She said she'd been worried about me. "Why should you worry yourself about me?" I said. "You're not dependent on me. And it was only a little two–day trip."

We emptied the money from the cycle bag into the black chest, and it filled it – indeed more than filled it: we couldn't even close the lid. It didn't help when we shook the money out of the blue mitten with the stars on and threw the mitten out of the window, or when I lifted Paula up to tread it down. We rang Nico. He came a few minutes later with two long leather straps, the sort that soldiers use to tie round boxes of ammunition. Then, with difficulty, we were able to close the lid.

The plastic surgeon came in the evening. We talked for a while about an area of very low pressure with storm-force gusts on its way from the west. And about everything else that lay before us. Then they wanted to be alone. I shut myself in my room and lay on the bed. My whole body ached, it wasn't used to work any more.

I lay there thinking about what had happened the first time I saw Paula; she was two or three days old and she made me so happy that I decided to return to childhood and relive it in her company. And before I went to sleep I had transposed myself back to that evening a long time ago, someone was reading aloud an article from *Swedish Women's Weekly* about the Prince of Monaco, and I could even hear Paula's father sitting down at the piano and bawling out at the top of his voice: "*Ritorna vincitor!* Restore to me my country, my palace, and the illustrious name that here I'm forced to hide!"

I N THE MORNING the area of low pressure had arrived. There were near-blizzard conditions and sleet as we carried down our small amount of luggage and stowed it in the boot of the limousine. I brought out the black chest last: that was going to travel on the back seat with us.

When we got to the northern edge of Stockholm city centre the car stopped and the nurse put blindfolds over our eyes. The snow was falling so thickly now that only the ground floors of the buildings could be seen. The Wenner-Gren Centre could have been any height, perhaps even infinite. That was the last thing we saw.

Then we disappeared. It's not really anything especially remarkable. Ten thousand Swedes disappeared after the Second World War. Paula's father and nine thousand nine hundred and ninety-nine others. No one can understand where they might have gone.

We soon left the motorway, and could no longer hear other cars. We bounced along on small bumpy winding roads, the chauffeur driving carefully in the new snow. I imagined to myself that I could hear the forest sighing. We said nothing, we were probably both anxious not to endanger this little adventure. We stopped after a few hours and the nurse brought out a bag of food she had with her and we ate in the car with our eyes still bound, which was quite difficult.

I don't know what time we arrived. He was already there, waiting for us. He and Paula hugged one another – I couldn't see them but I heard it. Only when we got to our rooms were we allowed to remove the blindfolds. Through the window I could see out over a park, covered in snow, and in the bay below there were two white swans swimming on the black water. Dusk fell as I stood there. I had put the black chest in my wardrobe.

We ate dinner in one of the small intimate dining-rooms. I don't know how many such dining-rooms there were in the manor house. It was just he and I and Paula. There were four landscapes by Elias Martin on the walls.

Afterwards we took our wine glasses and sat in a lounge with gigantic picture windows, and two spotlights shone on the elm and lime trees outside. I was drinking wine too, and would start doing so seriously from now on.

"Schopenhauer sometimes stayed with a friend who had an estate outside Weimar," I said. "He would sit under an oak and play the flute. 'I myself become so handsome and stately in these surround-ings,' he used to say."

"I didn't know that he had any friends," said Paula.

"What did he look like?" asked the plastic surgeon. "Schopen-hauer."

"He was the ugliest philosopher that's ever lived," I said. "His family came from Holland. It's sad to have to say it, but what he most resembled was an ape."

"People really don't have any objective appearance," said the plastic surgeon. "Appearance is merely something we imagine."

We drank to Schopenhauer.

After a while I could begin to make out a little building right down by the shore.

"What's that?" I asked, pointing.

"That's my little chapel," he said. "I built it mainly for myself. But it's always open to anyone."

He threw back his head to move the forelock that kept falling down over one eye.

Everything in this account is the truth. But in his case I have altered various things. No one must be able to recognise him, no one must be able to accuse him of anything. He didn't look as I've described him, he didn't resemble Klaus Mann in Dardel's draw-ing, and the forelock is my invention. His clinic in Stockholm is not on the street I mentioned. Though the manor house we were sitting in is true.

When he'd pushed his hair back into place he said: "I sometimes think that everything we create or assimilate is just some kind of reflection. Our actions represent our own selves. The chapel and the whole of this establishment are part of my appearance."

We were drinking white port.

"That sounds a bit complicated," I said. "Or abstract. I thought you were primarily interested in solid concrete matters."

"Yes," he said. "I'm only a simple craftsman. Even if I am the best in Sweden. I could equally well have been a picture-frame maker. But I'm always looking for ideas and philosophies to give status to my dexterity. And make it grander than it really is."

"Christianity," I said.

"Now don't be silly," said Paula.

"Yes," he said. "Conversion. Becoming a new person. Rebirth. I've thought of that."

"Your craftsmanship simply represents your faith," I said.

"Yes," he said. "That's how it is."

"For Paula and me," I said, "everything is just a whim. A fleeting thought and no more. We have to spend our money on something."

He actually didn't want to let us pay, he begged to be allowed to do it free, as a present for Paula. But we finally made him accept a plastic carrier bag of money. That enabled us to close the lid of the black chest and throw away the leather straps.

I told him the story of my grandfather's pianos. He said he would do his utmost to find one of them; it would really be the perfect instrument for this place, he said.

We talked an exceptional amount in all the months we stayed with him. There was nothing else to do. No newspapers, no radio or TV, the outside world didn't exist. We never even caught a glimpse of the other patients who must have been there.

After a few days it became difficult to talk, because we were completely swathed in dressings and bandages; we only had little slits to look out of and a small round opening for the mouth. We were given tablets to help against the pain. We couldn't swallow anything other than gruel and soup and wine. We started talking in a new way, restricted and child-like, and we simply couldn't manage some consonants at all.

One evening I had gone down to sit in the little chapel. Then he came. He sat down beside me. There was no altar, just a copy of Perugino's *Vision of St Bernard*.

"This Christianity," I puffed and lisped through the tiny hole in the bandages, "what does it really mean to you?"

He took a good while to answer. His explanation was long and detailed. Greatly abridged, this is roughly what he said: "It's built up on an infinite number of ideas, each more crazy and absurd than the others, and if you examine them one by one you find nothing to believe in. But taken all together, those ideas given an absolutely true concept of life."

I think I understood what he meant. And for a thousandth of a second I too was a Christian.

On another evening we were standing out on the terrace listening to what he told us was an eagle owl, he and I and Paula, when he said: "You never know how this sort of decision evolves. Once I come on the scene there's never any going back."

He was talking about Paula and me.

"It's become an absolute necessity," said Paula. "There's something we have to escape from, God knows what it is. Chance, or something like that."

"Roy Charles Sullivan was struck by lightning seven times," I said. "He was called the living lightning conductor from Virginia. He lost his nails and eyebrows and hair and had one foot cut off."

"For God's sake," said Paula. "Where can we turn?"

After six weeks we were to be freed from our bandages. He did it himself.

It took an hour or so. I had to lie on the bed in my room. He left me alone afterwards with my mirror. It was fantastic. I was totally unrecognisable.

Then he went on to Paula. She's told me about it.

She also had to lie down. He unwrapped the bandages so slowly and carefully that she felt nothing, it was actually as if he were doing something else altogether. He brushed his thumbs lightly over the scars. Then he straightened up and looked at her.

When he had stared long enough he put his hand over his eyes. The cotton bandages lay in a heap at his feet. He went over to the window and gazed out at the park. Finally he cleared his throat and said:

"I can't help it. I've really tried my hardest. But with the best will in the world I can no longer love you."

But she wasn't listening to him. Or she didn't care. She was already standing in front of the mirror stroking herself over the forehead and cheeks with both hands and pinching her new chin and laughing so uncontrollably that even I could hear her, though my room was at the other end of the corridor.

We ate lunch together. We tried to pretend that everything was as usual. I recognised Paula by her voice and her fingers that had to play with something all the time, her knife and fork and glass and bread. I think he'd had Botticelli's *Venus* in mind when he modelled her new face. Every line and shading was perfect. She hardly gave herself time to eat, she couldn't tear her eyes away from my new and manly face and my curly hair. At last she was seeing me as I really am.

He obviously noticed how impatient and distracted we were. He said nothing. As he ate, concentratedly and somewhat mechanically, he just stared down at his plate. As soon as the dessert came, we told him we would like to be alone. If he wouldn't be offended. If it wasn't too brazen of us.

And then we said it straight away, almost taking each other's words out of our mouths. She loved me and I loved her.

Once that was settled we sat in silence for a long time. Paula had rolled a ball of bread, and she pushed it in between my full and well-formed lips.

Not even the brandy that was served with the coffee could get us talking as we once had, the way our old, cast-off personae used to talk.

We exchanged only a few words. It was fine, we said. It was really practical and convenient that we were in love with each other. It was of course an absolute necessity and essential prerequisite if everything was to have a proper happy ending.

A week later the scars had faded and disappeared. We were ready to set off.

Everything was arranged. We had new names and personal identity numbers. And passports. And income tax assessments, Co-op membership cards, insurance certificates and identity discs. Everything that makes us human beings.

We came here. The sound of the sea is gentle on the ear and at just the right distance. Paula can sing as loudly as she wants without anyone hearing her. We can be ourselves at last. All the time. Every morning I mix a *Für Immer Selig* in a two-litre demijohn. Sometimes I play *"O Sole Mio"*. The countryside looks like a genuine oil painting by Ström. It's a world which is entirely will and idea. The birds sing for an hour in the evening and an hour in the morning. The cherry tree is in blossom. And the peach tree. When they're not in blossom they're bearing fruit.

I have written this account using the upturned black chest as a desk. Now as I finish and gather up my papers, my grandfather's scrolled letters come into view again. In fact I needn't have bothered with all this writing, I could have been content with the message he had carved with his knife:

PRAISED BE THE LORD

Harvill Paperbacks are published by Harvill,
an Imprint of HarperCollinsPublishers

For the full list of titles please write to:

Harvill/HarperCollins*Publishers*,
77–85 Fulham Palace Road, London W6 8JB
enclosing a stamped self-addressed envelope